Where Tides Meet

Kenneth Thomas

Published by Kenneth Thomas, 2024.

This is a work of fiction. Similarities to real people, places, or events are entirely coincidental.

WHERE TIDES MEET

First edition. December 2, 2024.

ISBN: 979-8230475682

Written by Kenneth Thomas.

Also by Kenneth Thomas

Harrow Harbor Mysteries
Whispering Harbor Mystery
The Secret of the Cavern
The Ghost Ships Shadow

Moonlight Pact series
The Moonlight Pact
The Rift Redemption
The Riftbound Legacy

The Awakening Thread Chronicles
The Awakening Thread

The Broke Kids Club
The Broke Kids Club
The Broke Kids Club: Ripples of Change

The Broke Kids Club Collection
The Broke Kids Club Collection

The Convergence of Minds series
The Digital Agora: A Philosophical Epic of AI and Humanity
Foundation of the Agora
Beyond the Agora: Fractured Realms

The Echoes of Eternity
The Awakening of Nephira
The Rift Of Worlds

The Eclipse Chronicles
Shards of Light
Eclipse Reaver
Axis Reforged

The Veil of Shadows Series
Shattered Dominion
The Fractured Path

Standalone
A Tail of Darkness To Light

The Mirror Within
Echoes of Ink and Heart
Purpose Over Power: The Visionary Path of Servant Leadership
The Questions That Shape Us: Finding Life's Wisdom-The Power of
Inquiry
Where the Shadows Settle
30 Days to Inner Freedom: A Mindful Journey in Addiction Recovery
Towards a Sustainable Future: The UN's 17 Goals
Echoes of Becoming
Cognitive Freedom: The Stoic Path to Resilience and Recovery
Beneath the Cypress Sky
The Unbroken Pen
Where Tides Meet

Where the Tides Meet
By Kenneth Thomas

Chapter One: A Stormy Homecoming

The rain slashed against the windshield like nature's own vendetta. Isla Merrick gripped the steering wheel tighter, her knuckles white as she squinted through the distorted view of Windhaven's coastal road. It was as though the town itself were testing her resolve, throwing gale-force winds and torrential rain her way, whispering, Turn back. You don't belong here anymore.

She ignored it, pushing her battered station wagon forward. Windhaven had been her home once. A sanctuary before the cracks of family betrayal and whispered gossip splintered her life into jagged pieces. Ten years away hadn't dulled the sting of her father's scandal, or the way the town had turned on her mother, on her.

Ahead, the outline of The Tidesong Inn came into view, silhouetted against the stormy sky. The sight of it struck her like a punch to the chest. It looked both smaller and sadder than she remembered, its once-pristine white paint now peeling in strips that flapped in the wind like surrender flags. The wrought-iron sign hanging above the porch swayed precariously, creaking with a sound that sent a chill through her.

A flash of lightning illuminated the towering oak at the edge of the property. Its gnarled branches stretched toward the heavens like a skeletal hand. Just as Isla's car rolled into the driveway, a thunderous crack rent the air. One massive branch snapped free, crashing down with startling force.

Isla slammed on the brakes, her heart leaping into her throat. The branch hit the hood of her car with a deafening crunch, splintering wood and shattering her already fragile nerves. She sat frozen, the storm raging around her, rain hammering against the roof as her breath came in shallow gasps.

"Perfect," she muttered, her voice shaking. "Welcome home, Isla."

The car door groaned in protest as she forced it open, the wind catching it and nearly wrenching it from her grasp. Rain soaked through her sweater in seconds as she stepped out, surveying the damage. The branch was thick, its jagged edges resting like a warning across the hood of her car. She touched the metal, her fingers trembling.

"You've got to be kidding me," she whispered, the words nearly swallowed by the howling wind.

"Move!"

The shout came from somewhere behind her, rough and commanding. Isla whirled around to see a man striding toward her, his figure cutting through the rain like an unstoppable force. His flannel shirt was drenched, clinging to broad shoulders, and his boots splashed through the mud with purpose.

"What—" she began, but he was already next to her, gripping the branch and heaving it off the car with a strength that left her momentarily speechless.

"Are you trying to get yourself killed standing out here like that?" he barked, his voice sharp enough to slice through the storm.

Isla bristled, the words snapping her out of her daze. "I wasn't standing here for fun!" she shot back, the indignation in her tone a defense against the flutter of panic still lingering in her chest.

The man straightened, tossing the branch aside as though it weighed nothing. His face came into focus under the dim glow of the inn's porch light, and Isla's breath caught. Strong jaw, high cheekbones, a ruggedness that spoke of someone who spent more time outdoors than in. His piercing blue eyes narrowed at her, assessing, as though she were some kind of puzzle he had no interest in solving.

"You should've called someone to check this place before you came back," he said, brushing rain from his forehead. "The storm's been rough on the old properties around here."

Isla squared her shoulders, refusing to let him see how rattled she was. "I didn't realize I needed a welcome committee."

His brow furrowed, and for a moment, his gaze softened. "You're Eleanor's granddaughter."

She blinked. "You know my grandmother?"

"Everyone knows Eleanor," he said, his voice dipping into something almost gentle. Almost. "She called me last week about some repairs."

"Oh." Isla shifted, the weight of his scrutiny pressing down on her. "And you are?"

"Callum Drake," he said. "Contractor. I do most of the restoration work around here." He glanced at the inn, his jaw tightening. "Looks like I've got my hands full with this place."

Isla bit back a sharp retort. She hadn't even stepped foot inside, and already someone was judging her ability to handle the task she'd taken on. "I'll manage," she said, forcing a smile that didn't reach her eyes. "But thanks for your... concern."

Callum's mouth twitched, though whether it was amusement or annoyance, she couldn't tell. "You've got a lot of work ahead of you. Better get started."

With that, he turned and strode away, leaving her standing in the rain, her pulse pounding for reasons she didn't want to examine too closely. She watched him disappear into the storm, his figure swallowed by the shadows, before turning back to the inn.

The porch steps creaked under her weight as she climbed them, water pooling beneath her boots. She hesitated at the front door, her hand hovering over the tarnished brass handle. The Tidesong had been her grandmother's pride and joy, a beacon for travelers seeking refuge by the sea. Now, it looked as though it were holding its breath, waiting to see if she was truly up to the task of saving it.

Isla squared her shoulders and pushed the door open.

The inside was worse than she'd imagined. Dust coated every surface, and the air was thick with the scent of mildew and decay. The once-warm parlor, with its brick fireplace and mismatched armchairs, now felt cold and lifeless. Cobwebs hung like ghostly curtains in the corners, and the floorboards groaned beneath her step.

She let out a long breath, brushing rain-soaked hair from her face. "Home sweet home."

Her grandmother's voice echoed in her memory: The Tidesong is more than a building, Isla. It's a legacy. A place where people find what they didn't know they were looking for.

She wondered what, if anything, she might find here.

The sound of a truck engine starting jolted her from her thoughts. Isla glanced out the rain-streaked window just in time to see Callum's taillights disappearing down the road. For a moment, she considered running after him, asking for help, but the thought left as quickly as it came.

No. This was her burden to carry. She'd come back to Windhaven to prove something—to the town, to her grandmother, to herself.

And she wasn't about to let anyone, least of all a gruff contractor with an attitude, tell her otherwise.

Chapter Two: Beneath the Surface

Morning broke with a weak, gray light filtering through the salt-smeared windows of The Tidesong. Isla rolled over on the lumpy couch she'd claimed as her makeshift bed, groaning as the stiffness in her neck reminded her of the storm's unwelcome welcome the night before.

She rubbed her eyes and sat up, surveying the parlor in daylight. If last night's gloom had softened the inn's disrepair, the sun was merciless in exposing it. Peeling wallpaper curled away from the walls like forgotten love notes, and the wood floors bore scratches deep enough to suggest battles waged between furniture and time. A particularly aggressive vine of ivy had pushed through a crack in one of the window frames, as though nature itself were intent on reclaiming the building.

"Good morning, Tidesong," Isla muttered. Her voice echoed faintly, swallowed by the emptiness of the room.

The to-do list in her mind loomed large: inspect the inn, assess what could be salvaged, and, most daunting of all, call her grandmother to explain the state of things. Eleanor Merrick wasn't exactly known for her patience, and Isla dreaded the inevitable lecture about neglect and missed opportunities.

She grabbed her phone, scrolling through emails while reheating the coffee she'd bought at a gas station on the drive in. But as the coffee sputtered in the microwave and the scent of burnt cardboard filled the air, a name caught her eye in the inbox: Liam Carter.

Isla froze.

She hadn't seen his name in months, but there it was, bold and unignorable, staring back at her like a ghost from the past. Against her better judgment, she opened the message.

Isla,

I heard you're back in Windhaven. Let's talk.

No signature, no pleasantries—just Liam's typical bluntness.

"Of course you'd hear," she muttered, slamming the phone down. She could almost hear the Windhaven gossip mill grinding away. Liam was likely eager to insert himself into her plans, the way he always had been: charming, persistent, but ultimately self-serving.

A loud knock shattered her thoughts.

Startled, Isla set down her mug and made her way to the door. When she swung it open, she found Callum Drake standing on the porch, looking as unruffled as the night before. He held a toolbox in one hand, and in the other, a folded sheet of paper fluttered in the breeze.

"Morning," he said, his tone clipped but not unkind. "Thought I'd stop by and check the damage. Looks like you've got more than just a storm problem here."

Isla crossed her arms, leaning against the doorframe. "I don't remember asking for an inspection."

Callum arched an eyebrow. "You didn't. Eleanor did."

Of course she had. Isla stepped aside with a sigh. "Fine. Come in, but don't expect me to thank you."

He brushed past her, his boots leaving faint muddy imprints on the worn floorboards. As his eyes scanned the room, he let out a low whistle. "It's worse than I thought."

"Thanks for the vote of confidence," she said dryly, shutting the door against the chilly morning air.

He ignored her sarcasm, crouching to inspect the base of a window where water had pooled. "This frame's completely rotted. It's not just cosmetic—you've got structural issues here. The whole place needs reinforcing."

Isla felt her irritation rising, though she couldn't quite pinpoint why. "I didn't ask for a critique of the whole building. I've got it under control."

Callum stood, brushing dust from his hands. His blue eyes locked onto hers, steady and unyielding. "I've worked on properties like this my whole life. You don't 'control' something like The Tidesong—it controls you. And if you don't respect that, it'll swallow you whole."

She opened her mouth to snap back, but something about his tone stopped her. He wasn't mocking her, she realized. He was warning her.

"Why are you even here?" she asked instead.

Callum's jaw tightened, but he didn't look away. "Because Eleanor asked me to help. And because whether you like it or not, you're in over your head."

Isla bristled. "I've handled bigger challenges than this. You don't know me."

"No," he said quietly, his gaze lingering on her for a beat too long. "But I know this place. And I know what it takes to bring something broken back to life."

The words landed heavier than she expected, pulling at the edges of her resolve. Isla looked away, focusing on the cracked plaster of the wall instead of his piercing eyes. "I'm not broken," she said, more to herself than to him.

Callum didn't answer. Instead, he unfolded the sheet of paper he'd brought and placed it on the rickety coffee table. "This is a preliminary estimate. Supplies, labor, timeline. Take it or leave it."

She glanced at the list, her stomach sinking at the numbers scrawled across the page. "This is... a lot."

"It's honest," he said. "And it's a start. Think it over."

Before she could protest further, he was heading for the door. Isla followed him, unsure whether she wanted to stop him or shove him out. "Wait," she called as he reached the porch.

He turned, his hand resting on the doorframe.

She hesitated. "Why do you even care? You could've just ignored my grandmother's call."

Callum studied her, his expression unreadable. "Windhaven's a small town. When someone's drowning, you throw them a rope. Even if they don't want it."

With that, he was gone, leaving Isla standing in the doorway, the sound of his truck engine fading into the distance. She clenched her fists, a swirl of frustration and gratitude tightening in her chest.

She didn't want to need him. She didn't want to need anyone.

But as she looked back at the sagging walls of The Tidesong, the weight of her task pressing down on her, Isla knew she might not have a choice.

Chapter Three: Anchors and Echoes

The soft whir of a shop vacuum hummed in the background as Isla crouched on the parlor floor, her fingers brushing against the torn corner of a rug. She peeled it back, revealing a hardwood surface beneath, scratched and stained with years of use and neglect.

Beneath the layers of grime, she could see the potential. The wood had a warmth that could still shine through, a resilience that hadn't been entirely destroyed by time. It mirrored something in herself, though she wasn't ready to admit that yet.

The vacuum sputtered to a halt. Isla glanced up to find Callum standing in the doorway, one hand resting on his toolbelt, the other holding a clipboard. He looked at her, then at the half-peeled rug.

"Not a bad start," he said.

Isla raised an eyebrow. "Was that... almost a compliment?"

"Don't get used to it." He smirked faintly and stepped inside, his boots leaving a faint trail of dust in their wake. "I need to check the foundation next. If it's as bad as I think, you're looking at a bigger project than you bargained for."

"Great," she muttered, standing and brushing her hands on her jeans. "Because things weren't overwhelming enough already."

Callum tilted his head, his expression unreadable. "Why'd you come back, anyway? You don't strike me as someone who likes getting their hands dirty."

Isla crossed her arms, her defenses snapping into place. "And you don't strike me as someone who asks personal questions."

His smirk disappeared, replaced by a steady gaze that pinned her in place. "Fair enough."

He turned and headed toward the kitchen, leaving Isla feeling like she'd dodged a question she wasn't ready to answer.

The kitchen was a disaster, a relic of another era. The old gas stove looked as though it hadn't been used in decades, and a rusted faucet dripped steadily into the porcelain sink. Callum pulled open a cabinet door, wincing as the hinges creaked loudly.

"This place has been sitting empty too long," he said, his voice muffled as he crouched to inspect the pipes under the sink.

"It wasn't supposed to be like this," Isla said softly, more to herself than to him. She leaned against the counter, her eyes tracing the faded wallpaper patterned with yellowing daisies.

Callum emerged from under the sink, brushing dirt off his hands. "What do you mean?"

She hesitated, the weight of her memories pressing against her. "When I was a kid, this place was alive. People came here from all over—honeymoons, anniversaries, family vacations. My grandmother made everyone feel like they belonged, like they were part of something special." She shook her head, a bitter smile tugging at her lips. "And then it all fell apart. The scandal, my dad disappearing, my mom dragging me away in the middle of the night..."

Her voice trailed off, and she suddenly felt exposed, like she'd said too much.

Callum studied her for a moment, his expression softer than she'd expected. "Places like this... they take on the weight of the people who live in them. If you rebuild it, maybe you'll find some of that life again."

Isla blinked at him, caught off guard by the gentleness in his tone. "That was surprisingly poetic."

He shrugged, straightening. "Don't let it go to your head."

Before she could respond, a sharp knock echoed through the inn. Isla frowned. "Were you expecting someone?"

"No," Callum said, already moving toward the front door. Isla followed, her stomach tightening with unease.

When Callum opened the door, Isla's heart sank.

Liam Carter stood on the porch, his easy smile as polished as the navy blazer he wore. His hair was neatly styled, his shoes gleaming despite the muddy road outside. Everything about him screamed control, precision, and confidence—the antithesis of the chaos Isla currently lived in.

"Liam," she said, her voice flat.

"Isla," he replied, his tone warm, as if they were old friends reconnecting instead of ex-lovers with a messy history. His eyes flicked to Callum, his smile tightening. "And you must be the contractor."

Callum crossed his arms, his posture radiating quiet authority. "Callum Drake."

"Liam Carter," he said, extending a hand. When Callum didn't move to shake it, Liam dropped his arm, his smile never faltering.

"What are you doing here, Liam?" Isla asked, cutting through the tension.

Liam turned his attention back to her, his expression softening. "I heard you were back, and I wanted to see how you were doing. Thought you might need some help getting the inn up and running."

"I'm fine," Isla said quickly.

"You don't look fine." Liam's gaze drifted to the peeling paint on the walls, the warped floorboards, the general disarray. "This is a lot to take on by yourself."

"She's not by herself," Callum said, his voice low and firm.

Isla shot him a glance, surprised by the sudden note of protectiveness in his tone.

Liam raised an eyebrow, clearly amused. "Of course. I just meant she might need someone with... resources. Connections."

"Noted," Callum said curtly.

Isla stepped forward, placing herself between the two men. "Liam, thanks for stopping by, but I've got this under control."

"Isla," he said, his voice dropping into a smooth, persuasive tone she remembered all too well. "I know we didn't part on the best terms, but I still care about you. I want to help."

Something inside her twisted, a mix of anger and old hurt bubbling to the surface. "You didn't care when you walked away the first time," she said quietly.

Liam's smile faltered for the first time. "That was... complicated."

"No," she said, her voice firmer now. "It wasn't."

The silence that followed was heavy, the tension thick enough to cut.

Callum broke it with a dry, pointed tone. "I think she's made herself clear."

Liam's eyes narrowed slightly, but he nodded. "If you change your mind, you know where to find me."

He turned and walked back to his car, the sound of his polished shoes clicking against the porch. Isla let out a long breath as the car disappeared down the road.

"Old friend?" Callum asked, his voice laced with sarcasm.

"Something like that," Isla muttered, turning back toward the inn. "Let's just say Liam has a habit of showing up when it's convenient for him."

Callum didn't press her further, but as they stepped back inside, she could feel his gaze on her, steady and searching.

She shook it off, focusing instead on the task at hand. The Tidesong needed her attention, her energy, her determination. And she wouldn't let Liam—or anyone else—distract her from what she'd come here to do.

Chapter Four: Cracks in the Armor

The scent of sawdust filled the parlor as Callum drilled into one of the window frames, the rhythmic whir of the tool underscoring the silence between him and Isla. She sat cross-legged on the floor, a notepad in her lap, pretending to focus on the list of repairs she'd been drafting.

The truth was, she couldn't stop replaying Liam's visit in her mind. His sudden appearance had stirred up emotions she'd thought she'd buried: anger, regret, and that faint, unwelcome pang of nostalgia. But more than that, Callum's presence was throwing her off balance.

"Shouldn't you be working on something?" Callum's voice cut through her thoughts, low and rough, tinged with exasperation.

"I am working," she shot back, scribbling nonsense on her notepad for emphasis.

He didn't look up, but the faint smirk tugging at his lips was impossible to miss. "Making a list isn't working. It's stalling."

Isla huffed, her irritation bubbling over. "You know, for someone who's supposed to be helping, you're awfully judgmental."

Callum set down the drill and turned to face her, his eyes meeting hers with that unflinching intensity she was starting to find maddening. "I'm not here to hold your hand, Isla. If you want to save this place, you're going to have to do more than make lists."

Her cheeks flushed, heat rising from a mixture of embarrassment and indignation. "I'm not afraid of hard work," she said, standing abruptly. "I've done just fine on my own for the past ten years, in case you hadn't noticed."

He leaned back against the windowsill, crossing his arms. "And yet, here you are. Back in Windhaven, back at The Tidesong. Why is that, Isla?"

The question hit her like a wave, catching her off guard. For a moment, she couldn't find the words to answer. Instead, she stared at him, her defenses crumbling under the weight of his gaze.

"I—" She stopped herself, shaking her head. "It doesn't matter."

"It matters," Callum said, his tone softer now, but no less insistent.

Isla looked away, her eyes landing on the warped floorboards beneath her feet. "This place used to mean everything to my grandmother," she said quietly. "And to me. I thought maybe... maybe if I could bring it back to life, I'd feel like I belonged somewhere again."

Callum didn't respond immediately, but the silence felt less heavy, more understanding. When she finally looked up, his expression had shifted. The hardness was gone, replaced by something warmer, something she didn't dare name.

"You're not the only one trying to piece things back together," he said after a moment, his voice low.

Isla opened her mouth to ask what he meant, but before she could, the sound of a small, high-pitched voice called out from the porch.

"Dad!"

Both of them turned toward the door as it creaked open, revealing a little girl with curly blonde hair and an oversized raincoat. Her boots thudded against the floor as she ran inside, clutching a slightly damp paper bag.

"Lila," Callum said, his tone softening instantly.

"Grandma sent muffins!" the girl announced, holding up the bag triumphantly. Her eyes widened when she spotted Isla. "Oh! You're the lady fixing the spooky inn!"

Isla blinked, taken aback by the child's energy. "I guess that's me," she said, managing a small smile.

Lila bounded over, her curiosity shining brighter than the gloomy weather outside. "Dad said it was falling apart. Are you going to make it pretty again?"

"That's the plan," Isla said, crouching to meet the girl's gaze. "What do you think? Should I paint the walls pink?"

Lila wrinkled her nose. "Ew, no. Green. Like the sea."

Callum chuckled behind her, and Isla glanced over her shoulder, surprised by the sound. His face had softened entirely, his usual gruffness replaced by a quiet affection as he watched his daughter.

"Green it is," Isla said, turning back to Lila. "Thanks for the tip."

Lila beamed and darted back to her father, tugging on his hand. "Can I help, Dad? Please? I'll be careful."

Callum ruffled her curls. "Not today, kiddo. But maybe later, okay?"

She pouted but didn't argue, instead busying herself by exploring the parlor.

"She's... spirited," Isla said, standing and brushing off her jeans.

"That's one way to put it," Callum said, his lips quirking into a faint smile.

For a moment, the tension between them dissolved, replaced by something lighter. Isla found herself studying him, the way his guard lowered when he spoke to Lila, the way his smile transformed his face.

"You're good with her," she said before she could stop herself.

Callum looked at her, his expression unreadable. "She makes it easy."

Isla nodded, unsure how to respond. A part of her wanted to ask about Lila's mother, about the life Callum had before Windhaven's storms etched lines of grief into his face. But she didn't. It felt too personal, too raw.

Instead, she picked up her notepad and returned to her spot on the floor. "I'll, uh, keep working on this list," she said, her voice unnaturally bright.

Callum's gaze lingered on her for a moment longer before he turned back to the window. "You do that."

But as he picked up his drill again, Isla couldn't shake the feeling that they'd just crossed some invisible line, one that couldn't be uncrossed.

Chapter Five: The Weight of the Past

The air inside The Tidesong grew warmer as the day wore on, the scent of fresh sawdust mingling with the salty tang of the sea breeze slipping through the open windows. Callum was deep in work on the parlor window, his movements methodical and precise, while Isla worked on clearing the last remnants of her grandmother's forgotten possessions from the kitchen cupboards.

Despite the rhythm of activity, a strange quiet had settled between them—a silence not of tension but of something deeper, like both were afraid to disturb the fragile truce that had begun to form.

Isla pushed open the final cupboard door and stifled a groan at the clutter inside. Stacks of mismatched plates, a faded floral teapot, and a rusting tin labeled Tea greeted her. She pulled out the tin and opened it, only to find a small bundle of yellowed envelopes tied with a pale blue ribbon.

Her breath hitched.

She stared at the bundle for a moment, her hand hovering over it as if it might vanish. Finally, she untied the ribbon, her fingers trembling as she unfolded the topmost letter. The handwriting was unmistakable—her grandmother's looping script.

My dearest Isla, it began.

The ache in her chest was sudden and sharp. Isla hadn't expected to feel anything so potent, but there it was, an uninvited flood of memories washing over her. She scanned the letter, her heart pounding as her grandmother's words leapt off the page.

You have your mother's strength and your father's heart. I hope you know that no matter where you go, or what mistakes you think you've made, this place will always be waiting for you. You belong here, my love.

Isla clenched her jaw against the sudden prick of tears. Her grandmother had written this long before the scandal that had driven their family apart, long before Isla had run away and sworn never to look back.

"What's that?"

Callum's voice startled her, and she quickly folded the letter, slipping it back into the tin. "Nothing," she said too quickly, her voice tight. "Just some old papers."

He didn't move from the window, but his eyes lingered on her for a moment. "You've been quiet," he said, his tone carefully neutral.

"I'm busy," Isla replied, grabbing another stack of plates from the cupboard.

"Busy running," Callum said, matter-of-factly.

Isla froze, her fingers gripping the chipped ceramic. She turned to him, her eyes narrowing. "Excuse me?"

He set down his tools and leaned against the windowsill, crossing his arms. "You've been darting around this place all day, avoiding the hard stuff."

"I'm cleaning," she shot back, her voice rising. "That's what you do when you restore a place. You clean it."

He shrugged, unbothered by her tone. "Sure. But cleaning's easy. Facing what this place means to you? That's harder."

His words struck a nerve, sharp and precise. "You don't know anything about me," she snapped, her anger masking the rawness in her voice.

Callum stepped closer, his eyes steady and unrelenting. "I know what it looks like when someone's carrying the weight of the past on their shoulders. And I know what it looks like when they're trying to outrun it."

Isla's chest tightened, the truth of his words hitting her harder than she cared to admit. She turned away, her hands gripping the edge of the counter as she tried to steady herself.

"What do you want from me?" she asked finally, her voice low and strained.

"Nothing," Callum said quietly. "But maybe you need to figure out what you want for yourself."

The silence that followed was thick, almost suffocating. Isla stared down at the worn surface of the counter, her mind racing. She wanted to lash out, to tell him he was wrong, but the words wouldn't come.

Instead, she took a deep breath and said, "This isn't your problem."

"No," Callum said, his voice softer now. "But it is yours. And the sooner you stop running from it, the sooner you can figure out what you're really doing here."

He didn't wait for her response. He grabbed his tools and headed toward the front door, pausing just long enough to glance back at her.

"I'll be back tomorrow," he said. "Think about what I said."

And then he was gone, leaving Isla alone with the tin of letters and the weight of his words.

She stared at the door long after it closed, her chest tight with a mix of anger, shame, and something else—something she wasn't ready to name.

That evening, Isla sat on the floor of the parlor with the tin in her lap, the letters spread out around her like fragile artifacts of a life she'd tried to forget. Each one told a story: her grandmother's quiet resilience, her unwavering belief in the inn's magic, her hope that Isla would one day return and see it for herself.

But one letter stood out. Unlike the others, it wasn't addressed to Isla.

It was addressed to Isla's father.

Her hands shook as she unfolded the letter, her grandmother's words unraveling a thread of buried family secrets.

Michael,

You made your choices, and I've made peace with that. But Isla deserves better than the lies you've left in your wake. If she ever finds her way back here, I hope she finds the truth, too. She deserves to know what kind of man her father truly was.

Isla's breath caught. Her father's departure had always been a mystery cloaked in whispers and half-truths, but this letter hinted at something more. Something darker.

Her chest tightened as a fresh wave of questions flooded her mind. What truth had her grandmother been hiding? And what would it mean for Isla now that she'd found this?

As the last rays of sunlight faded behind the horizon, Isla felt the weight of the past pressing down on her like never before.

But this time, she couldn't ignore it.

Chapter Six: Foundations of Truth

The next morning dawned with an overcast sky, the kind of heavy gray that made it impossible to tell where the sea ended, and the horizon began. Isla stood in the kitchen, staring at the tin of letters on the counter. She'd barely slept, her mind tangled in the questions raised by the note addressed to her father.

The truth. Her grandmother had wanted her to know something about her father, something no one had ever told her. But why hide it in a letter? Why not just tell her?

A knock at the door broke through her thoughts, sharp and deliberate. Isla glanced at the clock—it was early, far too early for visitors. When she opened the door, she wasn't surprised to see Callum standing there, his toolbox in hand, looking as calm and implacable as ever.

"You're up," he said simply.

"Barely," Isla replied, stepping aside to let him in. "You're early."

"Work doesn't wait," he said, setting his toolbox on the floor of the parlor. His eyes flicked to her face, and he paused. "You look like you didn't sleep."

Isla ignored the comment, walking past him toward the parlor. "Let's just get started. What's on the agenda today?"

"Foundation inspection," he said, crouching near the corner of the room and pulling a pry bar from his box. "If the base of this place is solid, we can build on it. If not, you're looking at a much bigger problem."

His words hit closer to home than he likely intended. Isla folded her arms and leaned against the wall, watching as he worked. The silence stretched between them, heavy and charged.

"Do you always have to be so... straightforward?" she asked finally, her voice tinged with exasperation.

Callum glanced up at her, his expression steady. "Would you rather I lie to you?"

"No," she admitted, looking away. "I just—never mind."

He turned his attention back to the floor, prying up a loose board with a sharp crack. Beneath it, the foundation was visible: old stone, weathered but surprisingly sturdy.

"You got lucky," he said, brushing dirt from the edge of the stones. "This part of the foundation's held up well. Might need some reinforcement, but it's not as bad as it could be."

"Small mercies," Isla muttered, trying to focus on the practical instead of the whirlwind of thoughts spinning in her mind.

Callum sat back on his heels, his gaze shifting to her. "Something's on your mind."

"Nothing that concerns you," she said quickly.

"Doesn't look like nothing," he replied. "But suit yourself."

She hesitated, torn between wanting to keep the letter to herself and the strange pull she felt toward Callum's steady presence. Finally, she crossed the room and sat on the edge of the old sofa, the tin still sitting on the nearby table.

"My grandmother left me letters," she said, her voice quieter now. "One of them was to my father. It... mentioned something about the truth. Something he never told me."

Callum's hands stilled, his attention fully on her now. "What kind of truth?"

"I don't know," she admitted. "But I feel like she wanted me to find it. Like it's something important."

Callum leaned back against the wall, his expression thoughtful. "Secrets have a way of surfacing when you least expect them. If she left that letter for you, maybe she wanted you to decide whether you were ready to face it."

"Why does everything have to be so cryptic?" Isla said, a sharp edge of frustration creeping into her voice. "Why couldn't she just tell me?"

"Maybe she thought you'd come back here sooner," he said, his tone even. "Or maybe she didn't know how to say it herself."

The truth of his words settled heavily on her. She looked down at her hands, twisting them together. "I'm not sure I want to know."

"You do," Callum said, his voice certain.

Isla looked up at him, her brow furrowing. "How can you be so sure?"

"Because you're still here," he said simply.

The words hung in the air between them, and for the first time, Isla felt a faint glimmer of clarity. He was right—despite the mess, despite the doubts, she'd chosen to stay. And maybe that meant she was ready to face whatever her grandmother had hidden.

Later that afternoon, Isla found herself in the attic, a flashlight in hand and dust motes swirling in the dim light. The wooden beams creaked faintly beneath her feet as she navigated the maze of forgotten trunks and boxes, each one a potential Pandora's box of family history.

She opened the first trunk and rifled through its contents: old quilts, faded photographs, and a collection of seashells carefully arranged in a tin. It was strange, seeing pieces of a life that felt both familiar and foreign.

In the second trunk, she found a small leather-bound journal, the edges worn and the clasp rusted shut. She hesitated before prying it open, the faint scent of aged paper wafting up as she flipped through the pages.

Her grandmother's handwriting filled the pages, neat and deliberate. Most of the entries were mundane—notes about guests, weather reports, and small town gossip—but one entry caught her attention.

July 15th

Michael came by the inn today. He looked... nervous. Said he was leaving town for good, but he wouldn't say why. I pressed him, but he just kept saying it was for the best. I don't know what to think. He's my son, but sometimes I wonder if I ever really knew him at all.

Isla's pulse quickened. The entry was dated just weeks before her father disappeared, leaving their family in ruins. What had driven him away? And what had he been hiding?

Her grip tightened on the journal as her mind raced. This wasn't just about her father—it was about the inn, about her family, about the tangled web of choices and consequences that had brought her back to Windhaven.

The truth felt closer now, just out of reach. And for the first time, Isla felt a flicker of resolve burning through her doubts.

She wasn't leaving until she uncovered it all.

Chapter Seven: The Edge of Secrets

The wind had shifted overnight, sweeping in a brittle chill that carried the scent of seaweed and rain. Isla stood in the attic, the leather-bound journal balanced on her palm. The faint creak of the floorboards beneath her feet mirrored the unease swirling in her chest.

Her grandmother's words echoed in her mind. *Sometimes I wonder if I ever really knew him at all.*

Michael Merrick, the enigmatic father who'd vanished from her life, leaving behind unanswered questions and a legacy of whispers, had always been a figure of contradictions. Charming but distant. Warm but secretive. The journal painted him in the same shades of mystery, and Isla wasn't sure whether she felt closer to understanding him or further away.

A sharp knock on the front door broke her train of thought. She snapped the journal shut, shoving it into her bag before heading down the narrow attic staircase.

When she opened the door, Callum stood on the porch, a coil of rope slung over his shoulder and a toolbox in hand. His expression was unreadable, but his presence filled the space with a quiet steadiness that Isla was beginning to rely on more than she cared to admit.

"You're late," she said, trying to sound lighthearted, though her voice carried a faint edge.

"You're impatient," he replied evenly, stepping inside. His boots left faint marks on the worn floorboards as he glanced around. "How's the attic?"

Isla hesitated, clutching the strap of her bag. "Dusty. A lot of old junk, some keepsakes. Nothing worth writing home about."

Callum's sharp blue eyes settled on her, and Isla shifted under his gaze. "You sure about that?"

"What's that supposed to mean?" she asked, crossing her arms.

He shrugged, setting down his tools. "Just that you've got a look. Like you found something that matters."

Isla opened her mouth to protest but stopped herself. The journal felt heavy in her bag, its presence a secret she wasn't sure she wanted to share yet. "Maybe I did," she admitted finally, her voice quieter. "But I'm still figuring out what it means."

Callum nodded, his expression softening. "Fair enough."

The silence between them lingered, but it wasn't uncomfortable. Isla found herself grateful for Callum's restraint—he didn't push, didn't pry. He simply let the moment breathe.

The day's work was physically demanding. Callum spent hours reinforcing the foundation in the parlor while Isla worked on stripping the old wallpaper in the hallway. They didn't speak much, each absorbed in their respective tasks, but the occasional shared glance or passing comment bridged the quiet.

By mid-afternoon, Isla had peeled back enough wallpaper to reveal a patch of painted wood beneath. The color was faded, but the rich emerald green reminded her of the sea, and a faint smile tugged at her lips.

"What's so funny?" Callum asked, his voice startling her out of her thoughts.

She turned to find him standing in the doorway, his arms crossed and a faint sheen of sweat on his brow. "It's not funny," she said. "I just like this color. It's... calming."

Callum stepped closer, inspecting the wall. "Sea green," he said. "Good choice."

"You think so?"

He nodded. "This place needs something that ties it to where it belongs. The sea's part of its story."

Isla tilted her head, studying him. "You talk about this place like it's alive."

"It is," he said simply, his gaze drifting to the window. "Buildings like this have souls. They carry the weight of the people who've lived in them, worked on them. It's not just wood and stone."

She blinked, caught off guard by the unexpected poetry in his words. "You're full of surprises, you know that?"

Callum chuckled softly, the sound low and warm. "You think you've got me all figured out?"

"Not even close," she admitted, a faint smile playing on her lips.

Their eyes met, and for a moment, the air between them felt charged, electric. Isla's heart thudded in her chest, and she quickly looked away, picking at a stubborn scrap of wallpaper to distract herself.

Callum lingered for another moment before stepping back toward the parlor. "We'll need to talk about the next steps soon," he said, his tone more businesslike now. "There's a lot to decide."

"Right," Isla said, her voice steadier than she felt.

That evening, after Callum had left for the day, Isla sat in the kitchen with the journal open in front of her. She flipped through the pages, searching for more clues about her father's departure.

One entry caught her eye:

July 22nd

Michael came back today. He was frantic, said he had to leave town immediately. He wouldn't tell me why, only that it was dangerous for him to stay. I begged him to stay for Isla's sake, but he wouldn't listen. He left her a note, though. Said it was in the oak chest in the attic.

Isla's pulse quickened. The oak chest. She remembered seeing it earlier, tucked away in the corner of the attic beneath a pile of old linens. She hadn't thought to open it.

Without hesitation, she grabbed a flashlight and headed back up the narrow staircase. The attic was even colder at night, the wind rattling faintly against the roof. Isla crossed the room, her steps quick and purposeful, until she reached the chest.

She knelt down and pried open the heavy lid, the hinges groaning in protest. Inside, a small wooden box sat nestled among a tangle of blankets. Her hands trembled as she lifted it out.

The box was unadorned except for a simple brass latch. Isla opened it carefully, her breath catching as she saw what was inside: a folded piece of paper, yellowed with age, and a small, tarnished compass.

She unfolded the paper with delicate fingers. Her father's handwriting stared back at her, bold and deliberate:

My sweet Isla,

If you're reading this, it means I'm gone. There's so much I wish I could explain, but the truth is dangerous. All I can tell you is this: trust your instincts, and trust the sea. It will guide you where you need to go. The compass is yours now. Use it wisely.

Tears blurred her vision as she read the words again, trying to make sense of their cryptic meaning. The truth was dangerous? Trust the sea? What had her father been caught up in that would lead him to leave such a mysterious message?

She stared at the compass, its needle pointing steadily north, and felt a strange mix of fear and determination settle in her chest.

Whatever her father's secrets were, she was going to uncover them.

And she was starting to think The Tidesong held more of the answers than she ever could have imagined.

Chapter Eight: Compass of Memories

The compass lay heavy in Isla's palm, its tarnished surface glinting faintly under the flashlight's beam. She traced her fingers along its smooth edges, trying to make sense of her father's cryptic words. Trust the sea? What did that even mean?

Her mind raced with possibilities, each one more frustratingly vague than the last. She wanted to scream, to demand answers from the empty attic that only echoed with the creaks of its weathered beams.

The note and the compass felt like breadcrumbs leading her to an invisible trail. The more she tried to piece it together, the more tangled it all became.

The next morning, Isla found herself standing on the cliffside just beyond The Tidesong's property. The waves crashed against the rocks below, the sound rhythmic and relentless. The air smelled of salt and possibility. She clutched the compass tightly, her thumb running over its surface as if it might spring to life and point her toward the answers she sought.

She didn't hear Callum approach until he was standing a few feet away, his hands shoved into the pockets of his jacket. "You're up early," he said, his voice cutting through the morning stillness.

"So are you," she replied without turning to face him.

"Comes with the job," he said. "What about you? You don't seem like the type who wakes up at dawn for the view."

She finally glanced at him, his blue eyes sharp but not unkind. "Just... thinking."

He nodded toward the compass in her hand. "What's that?"

Isla hesitated, torn between the instinct to guard her father's message and the nagging feeling that Callum might actually understand the weight of it. "It's my father's," she said eventually. "I found it in the attic."

Callum stepped closer, his gaze fixed on the small object in her hand. "Looks old. Does it work?"

"Seems like it," Isla said, turning the compass over. "But it came with this note, and..." She trailed off, shaking her head. "It doesn't make any sense. It's just a bunch of cryptic nonsense about trusting the sea."

Callum frowned, his brow furrowing as he studied the compass. "Your dad was a sailor or something?"

"No," Isla said. "At least, not that I know of. He was an accountant—or at least that's what he told us. But now..." She sighed, tucking the compass into her pocket. "Now I don't know what to believe."

Callum watched her for a moment, his expression thoughtful. "Sometimes people keep secrets because they're trying to protect you. Doesn't make it right, but it's not always about hiding something bad."

Isla crossed her arms, turning her gaze back to the sea. "He left us," she said quietly. "Whatever he thought he was protecting us from, it wasn't enough to make him stay."

The words hung in the air, heavy and unyielding. Callum didn't try to fill the silence, and Isla found herself strangely grateful for it.

"Whatever he was running from," Callum said finally, his voice steady, "maybe you're not supposed to run from it anymore."

Isla turned to look at him, surprised by the certainty in his tone. "What makes you so sure?"

"Because you're here," he said simply.

The rest of the day passed in a blur of activity. Callum focused on stabilizing the damaged beams in the parlor, while Isla worked on sorting through more of the attic's clutter. Each discovery felt like a new thread in an unraveling tapestry—bits and pieces of her family's history that she hadn't realized were missing until now.

By late afternoon, she was exhausted, her arms sore from hauling boxes down the narrow staircase. She set the last one on the parlor floor, wiping her forehead with the back of her hand.

"Take a break," Callum said from across the room, his voice cutting through the quiet.

"I'm fine," she replied, even as she leaned against the wall for support.

"You're not," he said, setting down his tools and walking over to her. "You're running yourself ragged. Sit down for five minutes. That's an order."

Isla rolled her eyes but didn't argue, sinking onto the edge of the sofa. "You're bossy, you know that?"

"Comes with the territory," Callum said, smirking as he grabbed a bottle of water and handed it to her.

She took it, twisting off the cap and taking a long sip. For a moment, they sat in companionable silence, the distant sound of the waves filling the space between them.

"Why do you care?" Isla asked suddenly, her voice quiet.

Callum frowned, caught off guard by the question. "What do you mean?"

"I mean, why are you helping me?" she said, turning to look at him. "You don't have to. You could've just done the work Eleanor hired you for and left it at that."

Callum leaned back, his gaze steady as he considered her question. "Maybe I see something worth saving," he said finally.

Isla's breath caught, her chest tightening at the quiet intensity in his voice. She looked away, her fingers gripping the water bottle as she tried to ignore the way her heart was racing.

"Well," she said after a moment, her voice steadier than she felt, "thanks. I guess."

Callum didn't reply, but when she glanced at him again, there was a faint smile tugging at the corners of his lips.

That evening, as the sun dipped below the horizon, Isla found herself back on the porch, the compass in her hand. She turned it over, watching the needle spin before settling on north.

The sea stretched out before her, vast and unknowable, and for the first time, she felt a strange sense of connection to it—a pull she couldn't quite explain.

Trust the sea, her father had written.

And as the waves crashed against the shore, she wondered if maybe, just maybe, it was time to start trusting herself too.

Chapter Nine: The Sea's Whisper

The night wrapped The Tidesong in a cocoon of quiet, the only sounds the creak of its beams and the steady crash of waves against the cliffs below. Isla sat at the kitchen table, the compass resting on the weathered wood beside her. The journal lay open, its pages illuminated by the warm glow of a single lamp.

The more she read, the clearer it became that her father's departure wasn't a simple abandonment. Her grandmother's entries hinted at fear—of what, Isla couldn't tell—and an urgency that seemed to ripple through the lines.

Michael is convinced he has to leave. He says there are people looking for him. I don't know what he's gotten himself involved in, but it's not safe for him to stay.

Isla's fingers traced the edges of the page. The cryptic warnings and half-explanations left her with more questions than answers. What had her father done? Who had been after him? And why had he left her behind?

The compass glinted under the light, its needle quivering faintly as if attuned to something beyond her understanding. A thought struck her—an absurd one, but persistent nonetheless. What if her father's words weren't a metaphor? What if he really meant for her to trust the sea?

The next morning, Isla stood at the edge of the cliffs again, the wind tangling her hair and whipping the hem of her jacket. She held the compass in her hand, watching as the needle spun lazily before snapping northward.

"You're up here a lot," Callum's voice came from behind her, carrying over the sound of the waves.

Isla turned to see him approaching, his boots crunching against the gravel path. He had a way of moving that seemed deliberate yet unhurried, as though nothing could truly rattle him.

"Do you always sneak up on people?" she asked, arching an eyebrow.

"Only when they're distracted," he replied, a hint of a smirk tugging at his lips.

She gestured to the expanse of water stretching endlessly before them. "Just trying to make sense of this."

Callum's gaze shifted to the compass in her hand. "Still thinking about the note?"

"It's all I can think about," she admitted. "My dad wasn't exactly the poetic type, but this... It's like he wanted me to solve some kind of riddle. And I don't even know where to start."

Callum stood beside her, his presence solid and grounding. "Sometimes the answer isn't as far away as you think. Maybe it's right in front of you."

Isla frowned, turning the compass over in her hand. "You think this thing has the answers?"

"I think it might lead you to them," he said, his voice steady.

She stared at him, searching his face for any sign of teasing, but he was serious. "What would you do?" she asked softly.

Callum's gaze held hers, the wind tousling his dark hair. "I'd follow it."

By midafternoon, Isla was standing on the rocky beach below the cliffs, her boots sinking slightly into the damp sand. The compass needle pointed north, but there was no clear destination, no obvious path. The tide was out, revealing jagged rocks and tide pools glistening in the sunlight.

Callum had joined her, though he hung back, letting her take the lead. His quiet presence was comforting, a reminder that she wasn't entirely alone in this strange pursuit.

"What now?" she called over her shoulder, turning the compass in her hands.

"You tell me," he replied, his voice calm.

Isla sighed, scanning the shoreline. Then, something caught her eye—a narrow gap between two towering rocks, half-hidden by a tangle of seaweed. It didn't look like much, but something about it drew her in.

She stepped closer, the compass trembling faintly in her grip as she moved. The gap opened into a small cove, the walls of rock rising steeply on either side. At the center, a weathered wooden structure jutted out of the sand—a small boathouse, its roof partially caved in.

"Did you know this was here?" Isla asked, glancing back at Callum.

He shook his head, his expression unreadable. "No. But it doesn't look like it's been touched in years."

Isla's heart pounded as she approached the boathouse, her pulse quickening with every step. The door hung slightly ajar, the wood swollen from years of exposure to the elements. She pushed it open with a creak, the scent of salt and damp wood filling her lungs.

Inside, the light filtered through broken slats in the roof, casting uneven shadows on the floor. The space was small, empty except for a single wooden chest tucked into the corner.

Isla hesitated, her breath catching as she stepped closer. The chest was unremarkable, its edges worn and its latch rusted, but it felt significant. She knelt before it, her fingers trembling as she pried it open.

Inside was a bundle of papers, carefully wrapped in oilcloth to protect them from the damp. Isla unfolded them slowly, her eyes scanning the faded handwriting.

Callum stepped inside, his boots crunching softly against the sand-covered floor. "What is it?"

Isla's voice wavered as she read aloud. "It's... letters. From my dad."

Her hands shook as she flipped through the pages, the words revealing fragments of a life she hadn't known. Mentions of debts, of promises made and broken, of people he owed more than he could ever repay.

"He was running," she said finally, her voice breaking. "From something—or someone."

Callum crouched beside her, his presence solid and steady. "Do they say who?"

Isla shook her head, tears blurring her vision. "No. Just that he didn't want them to find us. That he thought leaving was the only way to keep us safe."

The weight of her father's choices pressed down on her, the realization settling like a stone in her chest. He hadn't left because he didn't care—he'd left because he thought it was the only way to protect her.

For a long moment, neither of them spoke, the sound of the waves filling the silence.

"You know," Callum said quietly, "running doesn't always keep people safe. Sometimes it just leaves them behind."

Isla looked at him, her heart aching at the truth in his words. "I don't know if I can forgive him," she admitted.

"You don't have to," Callum said. "But maybe understanding him is a start."

Isla nodded, clutching the letters tightly to her chest. The boathouse suddenly felt like a place suspended in time, a portal to a past she was only beginning to unravel.

For the first time in years, she felt like she was finally starting to find her way.

Chapter Ten: Fragments of Understanding

The letters spread out before Isla on the parlor table, their yellowed edges fragile against the smooth surface. Each one revealed a piece of the puzzle, fragments of her father's life she had never been privy to. Callum sat across from her, his posture relaxed but his eyes sharp, watching her as she sifted through the pages.

"He owed money," Isla said finally, her voice low and strained. "A lot of it. But it wasn't just that—there's something bigger here. He mentioned 'the syndicate' like it was some kind of shadow hanging over him."

Callum leaned forward, resting his forearms on the table. "Syndicate? That's not a term people throw around lightly. Sounds serious."

"It was," Isla said, brushing her fingers over one of the letters. "He talks about deals he couldn't fulfill, people he couldn't pay back. And then there's this..." She slid a letter across the table to Callum.

He picked it up, his expression darkening as he read aloud.

They're watching the house. I can't stay. If I'm gone, maybe they'll leave you and Isla alone. I'll find a way to make it right.

Callum set the letter down, his jaw tight. "This wasn't just about money. These people were dangerous."

Isla nodded, her throat tight. "And he thought running would protect us."

"It might have," Callum said carefully. "But it also left you without answers. Without him."

She looked away, her chest aching. "I spent so many years hating him for leaving. I thought he just... didn't care."

"And now?" Callum asked.

Isla exhaled slowly, the weight of her father's choices pressing down on her. "Now, I think he cared too much. He was willing to give up everything to keep us safe. But it doesn't make it hurt any less."

Later that day, Callum worked on reinforcing the front porch while Isla stood nearby, her thoughts swirling. The letters had given her a glimpse into her father's struggle, but they hadn't answered the most pressing question: why had her grandmother kept this from her?

"She must have known," Isla said, breaking the silence.

Callum glanced at her, his hammer poised over a nail. "Your grandmother?"

"She wrote about him in her journal. She knew he was in trouble, that he was running. But she never told me." Isla's voice wavered, frustration bubbling beneath the surface. "Why would she hide this from me?"

Callum set the hammer down, wiping his hands on a rag. "Maybe she thought you weren't ready to know. Or maybe she didn't have the whole story either."

Isla shook her head, pacing along the edge of the porch. "She had to have known more. The way she wrote about him—it's like she was carrying some kind of guilt. Like she thought she could have stopped him."

Callum stepped closer, his presence grounding. "What's stopping you from asking her?"

Isla froze, the thought lodging in her mind like a splinter. She hadn't called her grandmother since arriving at The Tidesong, partly out of avoidance, partly because she wasn't sure what to say. But now, the need for answers outweighed her hesitation.

"You're right," she said, pulling out her phone. "I need to talk to her."

The call connected after a few rings, Eleanor's voice crackling faintly through the line. "Isla? Is everything all right?"

"Hi, Grandma," Isla said, her voice tight. "I'm fine. I just... I found some things. Letters. From Dad."

There was a long pause on the other end. "I see," Eleanor said finally, her tone measured.

"They were in the attic," Isla continued. "Along with your journal. Why didn't you tell me? Why didn't you let me know what he was going through?"

Eleanor sighed, the sound heavy with age and regret. "Because I thought it was better that way," she said. "You were so young, Isla. I didn't want you to carry the weight of his mistakes."

"But they weren't just mistakes," Isla pressed, her voice trembling. "He was trying to protect us. From what? From who?"

"The syndicate," Eleanor said, her voice dropping. "Your father got involved with people he shouldn't have. He thought he could outsmart them, but when the debts came due, they didn't just want money—they wanted control."

"Control of what?" Isla asked, her heart pounding.

"The inn," Eleanor said. "The Tidesong has always been more than just a building. Your great-grandfather used it to smuggle goods during the war. Your father thought he could use those old connections to his advantage. But he was wrong."

Isla's knees buckled, and she sank onto the porch steps. "So this place... it's part of why he left?"

"Yes," Eleanor said softly. "And part of why I stayed. To make sure no one ever used it that way again."

The weight of the revelation pressed down on Isla like a tidal wave. The inn, her father's departure, her grandmother's silence—it was all connected, tangled in a history she was only beginning to uncover.

"Why didn't you tell me any of this?" Isla whispered.

"Because I wanted you to have a clean slate," Eleanor said. "But I see now that wasn't fair. I should have trusted you to decide for yourself."

Isla's grip on the phone tightened. "I need to know everything, Grandma. No more secrets."

Eleanor hesitated, then said, "Come see me. We'll talk. All of it."

As the call ended, Isla sat in stunned silence, the phone still pressed to her ear. Callum stepped closer, his expression cautious. "You okay?"

"No," Isla said honestly, standing on shaky legs. "But I'm starting to understand."

"Understand what?"

She turned to him, her eyes fierce despite the tears brimming in them. "That this place isn't just a part of my past. It's part of my father's story too. And if I want to move forward, I need to face it—everything he left behind."

Callum nodded, his steady gaze meeting hers. "Then let's face it."

For the first time, Isla felt a flicker of hope. The weight of the past was heavy, but with each step forward, it was beginning to feel just a little bit lighter.

Chapter Eleven: Roads to Revelation

The drive to Eleanor's home felt longer than it had any right to. The coastal highway twisted and turned with reckless abandon, each curve revealing glimpses of the sea glinting in the late afternoon sun. Isla gripped the steering wheel tightly, her mind racing with the weight of her grandmother's words.

The Tidesong isn't just a place—it's a legacy.

What did that mean? Her great-grandfather's smuggling operations, her father's debts, the syndicate—every piece of the puzzle seemed to center on the inn. Isla's chest tightened as she pulled into the gravel driveway of her grandmother's modest bungalow, the flower beds overgrown but still vibrant with color.

Eleanor was waiting for her on the porch, her sharp eyes watching as Isla stepped out of the car. Despite her frail frame and the lines etched deeply into her face, Eleanor Merrick still exuded an air of command.

"Isla," she said, her voice firm but warm.

"Grandma," Isla replied, her throat tight. She climbed the steps, and for a moment, they stood in silence, the gulf of unspoken words stretching between them.

Eleanor motioned toward the door. "Come inside. We have much to discuss."

The small sitting room smelled faintly of lavender and lemon polish. Isla perched on the edge of the floral-patterned sofa, clutching the compass in her hand like a lifeline. Eleanor settled into her armchair, her movements deliberate, her expression unreadable.

"You found the letters," Eleanor said after a moment, breaking the silence.

"I did," Isla said. "And I found Dad's compass. His note."

Eleanor's eyes flicked to the object in Isla's hand. "That compass belonged to your great-grandfather. He used it to navigate the coastline during his smuggling runs. Your father kept it as a reminder of where he came from—and what he thought he could leave behind."

"What exactly was he running from?" Isla asked, her voice trembling.

Eleanor sighed, her shoulders sagging under the weight of the truth. "Your father got involved with the wrong people—powerful people who controlled more than just money. The syndicate wasn't just after his debts. They wanted the inn because of its history, its location. They saw it as a perfect hub for their operations."

"And he thought leaving would protect us," Isla said, the bitterness in her voice unmistakable.

Eleanor nodded, her eyes glistening. "He was desperate. He thought if he disappeared, they'd lose interest in the inn and in us. But it wasn't that simple. After he left, they came to me."

Isla's stomach twisted. "What did they do?"

"They threatened," Eleanor said, her voice steady despite the tremor in her hands. "But I refused to give them the inn. I told them I'd rather burn it to the ground than see them take it. Eventually, they moved on, but I always feared they'd return."

The room fell silent, the weight of the past settling over them like a storm cloud.

"Why didn't you tell me?" Isla asked, her voice barely above a whisper.

Eleanor leaned forward, her gaze piercing. "Because I wanted to protect you. The less you knew, the safer you were. But now that you've come back, now that you've found the letters... I see I was wrong to keep it from you. You deserve to know the truth."

Isla swallowed hard, her mind spinning. The Tidesong wasn't just her grandmother's legacy or her father's refuge—it was a battleground, a symbol of defiance and survival.

"What am I supposed to do now?" she asked, her voice cracking.

Eleanor reached out, her frail hand covering Isla's. "You rebuild it. You make it yours. And you don't let anyone take it from you."

The drive back to The Tidesong felt different. The road was the same, the curves no less daunting, but Isla felt a new sense of purpose anchoring her. The inn wasn't just a relic of her family's past—it was her inheritance, her responsibility.

Callum was waiting for her on the porch, his figure silhouetted against the warm glow of the setting sun. He straightened as she pulled into the driveway, his eyes narrowing slightly as he studied her expression.

"You okay?" he asked as she climbed out of the car.

Isla nodded, though her mind was still racing. "I know what I need to do now," she said, her voice firm.

"Good," Callum said simply. "Then let's do it."

That night, Isla spread the letters and the journal out on the dining table, pouring over them with renewed determination. She mapped out connections, highlighting names and places that seemed significant.

Callum sat across from her, his quiet presence grounding. He didn't ask many questions, content to let her work through her thoughts aloud.

"The syndicate wanted the inn for its location," she said, tracing a line on an old map of the coastline. "These cliffs, the hidden coves—they're perfect for moving things without anyone noticing."

"But your grandmother stopped them," Callum said.

"For now," Isla replied. "But what if they come back? What if they still see the inn as a prize?"

Callum leaned back, his expression thoughtful. "Then we make it clear it's not for sale. Not to them, not to anyone."

Isla met his gaze, a flicker of gratitude sparking in her chest. "We?"

Callum shrugged, a faint smile tugging at his lips. "You're not in this alone, Isla. You've got people who care about you—your grandmother, the town... me."

Her breath hitched at his words, her chest tightening with a mix of emotion she couldn't quite name. For a moment, she allowed herself to lean into the steadiness of his presence, the warmth of his quiet support.

"Thank you," she said softly.

Callum nodded, his eyes holding hers for a beat longer than necessary. "We'll figure it out."

And for the first time since returning to Windhaven, Isla felt like maybe, just maybe, she could.

Chapter Twelve: A New Foundation

The next morning dawned crisp and golden, the kind of day that carried the promise of fresh starts. The Tidesong stood tall against the backdrop of the blue horizon, its weathered exterior bathed in soft sunlight. Isla stood on the porch, a steaming cup of coffee in hand, her mind buzzing with plans for the future.

She was done running, done letting the weight of the past dictate her choices. The Tidesong deserved more than survival—it deserved to thrive.

The sound of Callum's truck pulling into the driveway jolted her from her thoughts. She watched as he stepped out, his flannel shirt rolled to his elbows and a determined set to his jaw.

"Morning," he called, grabbing his toolbox from the truck bed.

"Morning," Isla replied, her lips curving into a faint smile. "Ready for another day of saving this place?"

Callum smirked, climbing the porch steps. "Always."

By midmorning, they were deep in the rhythm of work. Callum was in the parlor, replacing damaged beams, while Isla focused on sanding and priming the walls in what had once been the dining room. The scent of fresh wood and paint filled the air, a tangible reminder that progress was being made.

As Isla worked, her thoughts drifted to her grandmother's revelation. The syndicate, her father's departure, the inn's fraught history—it all felt surreal, like a story she'd read instead of a life she was living.

But as overwhelming as it was, Isla couldn't deny the flicker of pride she felt in being part of The Tidesong's story now.

Callum's voice pulled her from her reverie. "Isla!"

She set down her paint roller and hurried into the parlor, where Callum was crouched near one of the exposed beams. He looked up as she entered, his expression serious.

"What is it?" she asked, her heart skipping a beat.

"I found something," he said, gesturing to the beam.

Isla crouched beside him, her eyes widening as she saw what he was pointing to—a small, rusted tin wedged between the beam and the wall.

Callum worked it free, handing it to her carefully. Isla's hands trembled as she opened the lid, revealing a stack of folded papers and a small, intricately carved wooden figurine.

She unfolded the first paper, her breath catching as she recognized her father's handwriting.

To whoever finds this, the letter began. If you're reading this, it means The Tidesong has stood the test of time. I hid these here to protect the inn, to make sure its story is never forgotten.

Isla read on, her heart pounding as her father's words revealed a secret she hadn't anticipated. The figurine was a map key, carved to unlock a hidden compartment in one of the inn's original pieces of furniture. Her father had left it as a safeguard, a way to preserve the inn's true history while keeping it out of the wrong hands.

When she finished reading, Isla looked up at Callum, her chest tight with emotion. "He hid this here. He wanted to protect the inn, even after he was gone."

Callum nodded, his expression thoughtful. "Then it's up to you to finish what he started."

That evening, Isla and Callum worked together to find the hidden compartment described in her father's letter. The key led them to an old oak sideboard tucked in the corner of the dining room, its surface scarred but still sturdy.

Isla inserted the figurine into a small, nearly invisible notch in the sideboard's base. There was a faint click, and a hidden drawer slid open, revealing a collection of documents and an old, leather-bound ledger.

The ledger was filled with detailed accounts of her great-grandfather's smuggling operations, each entry meticulously recorded. But alongside the records were notes about the inn itself—how it had served as a haven for travelers and a lifeline for the community during lean times.

"This isn't just about smuggling," Isla said, running her fingers over the faded pages. "It's about the inn's role in the town's history. It was a symbol of resilience, of survival."

Callum leaned over her shoulder, his voice low. "And now it's your turn to carry that legacy forward."

Isla nodded, her resolve hardening. The Tidesong wasn't just a building—it was a living testament to her family's struggles and triumphs. She wouldn't let it be forgotten.

The next few days passed in a blur of work and determination. Word of Isla's efforts spread through Windhaven, and slowly, the townspeople began to rally around her. Neighbors stopped by to offer help, sharing stories of the inn's glory days and their own connections to its history.

Even Lila, Callum's daughter, pitched in, her enthusiasm and creativity breathing new life into the project. Together, they painted murals, repaired furniture, and prepared the inn for a new chapter.

One evening, as the sun dipped below the horizon, Isla stood on the porch with Callum, watching the waves crash against the cliffs. The inn behind them was beginning to look like its old self again, its spirit restored.

"Thank you," Isla said softly, her eyes fixed on the horizon.

Callum glanced at her, his expression warm. "For what?"

"For believing in this place. For believing in me."

He stepped closer, his voice low and steady. "It wasn't hard to do."

Their eyes met, the air between them charged with something unspoken. Isla's heart pounded as she searched his face, the weight of everything they'd been through together suddenly pressing down on her.

Before she could second-guess herself, she closed the distance between them, her lips brushing against his in a kiss that was both hesitant and certain.

Callum's hand came to rest lightly on her waist, anchoring her as the kiss deepened, the moment filled with the quiet promise of something new.

When they finally pulled apart, Callum smiled, his eyes shining with a mix of amusement and tenderness. "That was unexpected."

Isla laughed softly, her cheeks flushing. "I guess I'm full of surprises."

"I'm starting to notice," he said, his thumb brushing against her cheek.

As they stood together on the porch, the sound of the waves carrying their silence, Isla felt a sense of peace she hadn't known in years.

The Tidesong was more than a place—it was a beginning.

And so was this.

Chapter Thirteen: The Heart of the Tidesong

The early morning light bathed The Tidesong in a soft, golden glow. Isla stood in the dining room, running her fingers over the smooth surface of the restored oak sideboard. The hidden drawer had been carefully sealed again, the ledger and documents safely tucked inside until she could decide what to do with them.

For now, her focus was on the inn itself—its walls, its soul, and the people who had begun to rally around her in ways she hadn't expected.

The clang of tools from the porch pulled her from her thoughts. Callum's familiar silhouette was visible through the dining room window, his steady movements a calming presence. Isla grabbed her coffee and stepped outside, finding him bent over a section of the railing he was reinforcing.

"Morning," she said, leaning against the doorframe.

He glanced up, a faint smile playing on his lips. "Morning. Thought you'd sleep in for once."

She shook her head, grinning. "Not a chance. Too much to do."

"Good," he replied, straightening. "I was worried you'd decide to skip town now that you've put me to work."

"Tempting," she teased, "but I think I'll stick around. For now."

Callum chuckled, the sound low and warm, before returning to his work.

As the day progressed, more townspeople arrived to lend a hand. Mrs. Hensley, the owner of the local café, brought trays of sandwiches and lemonade, her chatter filling the air with stories of the inn's heyday. A group of teenagers from the high school helped scrub years of grime from the old garden statues, while a retired carpenter worked with Callum to restore the front doors.

The inn was alive with activity, laughter and purpose filling its once-silent halls.

Isla moved through it all, coordinating tasks and lending a hand where she could. But as the afternoon wore on, she found herself drawn to the cliffs, her father's compass once again nestled in her pocket.

She stood at the edge of the rocky outcrop, the wind tugging at her hair as she gazed out at the endless expanse of sea. The compass felt warm against her palm, its needle steady.

"I'm trying, Dad," she whispered. "I'm trying to understand. To make this place everything you wanted it to be."

The waves crashed below, their rhythm almost soothing. Isla closed her eyes, letting the sound wash over her. For the first time, she felt a flicker of connection—not just to her father, but to the generations of her family who had poured their lives into The Tidesong.

When she turned back toward the inn, she found Callum standing a few feet away, his hands in his pockets.

"You've got a habit of sneaking up on me," she said, though her voice lacked its usual bite.

"Not sneaking," he replied. "Just... keeping an eye on you."

Isla smiled faintly. "Well, I appreciate it. Even if you're terrible at giving me space."

Callum stepped closer, his gaze steady. "You don't really want space, do you?"

Her breath caught, her pulse quickening as the weight of his words sank in. She opened her mouth to respond but found she couldn't. Instead, she looked away, her fingers tightening around the compass.

"I think I've spent so long pushing people away, I don't know how to stop," she admitted finally.

Callum's voice was soft, steady. "Then maybe you just need someone who won't let you."

Isla turned to face him, her chest tight with a mix of fear and hope. "That sounds dangerous."

"Maybe," he said, his lips curving into a faint smile. "But some risks are worth taking."

She laughed softly, shaking her head. "You make it sound so simple."

"It can be," he said, stepping closer. "If you let it."

For a moment, Isla let herself lean into his warmth, the solid presence of him grounding her in a way she hadn't realized she needed.

"Thank you," she said quietly.

"For what?"

"For being here," she said. "For helping me believe this place can be something again."

Callum smiled, his eyes holding hers. "It already is."

The week passed in a blur of progress. The inn's exterior was repainted in a soft cream, its trim a rich sea green that mirrored the waves. The overgrown garden was cleared, revealing long-forgotten paths and flowerbeds. Inside, the parlor was transformed, its walls freshly painted and its furniture carefully restored.

Every corner of The Tidesong seemed to hum with new life.

One evening, as the final rays of sunlight bathed the cliffs in gold, the townspeople gathered in the garden to celebrate. Mrs. Hensley had brought a cake, and the teenagers strung fairy lights along the porch railings. Laughter and music filled the air, the inn's windows glowing warmly against the night.

Isla stood at the center of it all, her chest tight with gratitude.

"You did it," Callum said, appearing beside her with a drink in hand.

"We did it," she corrected, her smile soft.

He raised his glass in a silent toast, his eyes warm.

As the night wore on, Isla found herself drawn back to the cliffs, the distant sound of waves a comforting presence. Callum followed, his steps quiet but certain.

When they reached the edge, Isla turned to him, her heart full. "I think I'm starting to understand what home feels like."

Callum smiled, his gaze steady. "Good."

"Do you think it's possible?" she asked, her voice barely above a whisper.

"What's that?"

"To rebuild something that's been broken?"

Callum reached out, his fingers brushing hers. "I think it's the only way anything worth having gets built in the first place."

Isla's breath hitched, the weight of his words settling over her. She turned to him fully, her eyes searching his.

"I think you're right," she said softly.

And as the waves crashed against the cliffs below, Isla felt a quiet certainty settle in her chest.

The Tidesong wasn't just a place—it was a beginning.

And so was this.

Chapter Fourteen: Restorations of the Heart

The morning mist hung low over Windhaven, softening the edges of the town and blurring the line between land and sea. The Tidesong stood proudly in the misty light, its fresh paint glistening with dew. For the first time in years, the inn looked like a place full of promise.

Isla stood in the garden, her hands brushing the petals of a newly planted bed of lavender. The scent was calming, but her thoughts were anything but. The past few weeks had been a whirlwind of revelations, hard work, and emotions she was still untangling.

"Lost in thought again?" Callum's voice broke through the quiet, warm and familiar.

She turned to find him leaning against the porch railing, his hands shoved into his pockets. He was smiling faintly, but his eyes held a softness that sent a quiet thrill through her.

"Maybe," she admitted, standing and brushing the dirt from her hands. "There's a lot to think about."

"Like what?" he asked, stepping closer.

Isla hesitated, her gaze drifting toward the horizon. "Everything, I guess. The inn, my family, this... life I'm trying to build here."

"And?"

"And I don't know if I'm doing it right," she said, her voice barely above a whisper. "What if I mess it all up?"

Callum's hand brushed hers, grounding her. "You won't."

She looked up at him, her heart aching with the weight of everything she felt but couldn't say. "How do you know?"

"Because you're not the type to give up," he said simply. "And you're not in this alone anymore."

Isla's breath hitched, her chest tightening at the quiet certainty in his voice. She wanted to believe him, to let herself lean into the strength of his presence, but the fear of losing what they'd built still lingered.

"You make it sound so easy," she said, forcing a smile.

"It's not," he replied. "But it's worth it."

Later that afternoon, the inn was alive with activity. The last of the repairs were underway, with neighbors stopping by to offer their final touches. Lila was in the kitchen with Mrs. Hensley, helping bake cookies for the small gathering Isla had planned to celebrate the inn's rebirth.

As Isla moved through the halls, she couldn't help but marvel at how far they'd come. The Tidesong wasn't just a building anymore—it was alive, its walls humming with the energy of the people who had poured their hearts into it.

In the parlor, Callum was adjusting one of the newly hung light fixtures. He glanced down as Isla entered, his smile tugging at the corners of his lips.

"Looks like it's all coming together," he said, stepping off the ladder.

"It really is," Isla agreed, her voice tinged with awe.

Callum studied her for a moment, his gaze steady. "You should be proud of yourself."

She hesitated, then smiled softly. "I think I am."

"Good," he said. "Because you've earned it."

The warmth in his tone sent a shiver through her, and for a moment, Isla felt a quiet contentment she hadn't known in years.

That evening, the small celebration unfolded under the glow of string lights strung along the porch. Neighbors and friends gathered in the garden, their laughter mingling with the sound of the waves. Isla moved through the crowd, her heart full as she accepted hugs, compliments, and well-wishes.

At the edge of the garden, Callum stood with Lila, his easy smile softening as he watched Isla. When their eyes met, he gave her a small nod, as if to say, You did this.

When the crowd began to thin, and the lights grew softer against the encroaching night, Isla found herself standing by the cliff's edge once more. The horizon stretched endlessly before her, the sea glinting under the moonlight.

Callum joined her a moment later, his presence steady and grounding.

"You always end up out here," he said, his voice low.

"It's where I think best," she replied. "Something about the sea makes everything else feel... smaller."

"Not smaller," Callum said. "Just clearer."

She turned to him, her heart pounding as the weight of the moment settled between them. "You've been a big part of this, you know. I couldn't have done it without you."

"You could have," he said, his voice steady. "But I'm glad you didn't have to."

Isla's breath hitched, her chest tight with a mix of fear and longing. "Callum..."

He stepped closer, his gaze searching hers. "You don't have to say anything, Isla. I just want you to know—I'm here. For as long as you want me to be."

The vulnerability in his words broke something open inside her, and before she could second-guess herself, she reached for him, her hands curling into the fabric of his shirt as she kissed him.

It was soft at first, tentative, but the moment his arms wrapped around her, the kiss deepened, filled with all the emotions they'd been holding back.

When they finally pulled apart, Callum rested his forehead against hers, his voice a whisper. "I'm not going anywhere."

Isla closed her eyes, letting the truth of his words settle in her chest. For the first time in years, she felt like she could finally breathe.

The Tidesong had been rebuilt—its walls, its spirit, and the future it promised.

And maybe, just maybe, Isla had rebuilt herself along the way.

Chapter Fifteen: Love Anchored

The morning after the celebration dawned clear and crisp, the kind of day that made everything seem possible. Sunlight streamed through the windows of The Tidesong, casting golden patches on the newly polished floors. Isla stood in the dining room, holding a cup of coffee and soaking in the quiet triumph of the moment.

For the first time in years, the inn felt alive again—not just with activity, but with the warmth of hope.

She wandered into the parlor, where Callum was already at work repairing the final piece of furniture, an old rocking chair that had belonged to her grandmother. He looked up as she entered, his lips curving into the easy smile that had become so familiar.

"Couldn't stay away, huh?" he teased, setting down his tools.

"Guilty," Isla replied, leaning against the doorway. "I just wanted to see how it was coming along."

"Almost there," Callum said, brushing a bit of sawdust from his hands. "This chair's seen better days, but it's solid. Just needed a little care."

Isla smiled softly, her chest tightening at the quiet significance of his words. "That seems to be a theme around here."

Callum stepped closer, his expression warm. "You did it, Isla. The inn looks incredible. And you..." His gaze softened, lingering on her. "You look like you've finally found where you're supposed to be."

She glanced away, her cheeks warming. "I had a lot of help."

He tilted his head, his smile growing. "Not as much as you think. This place, this transformation—it's all you."

The sincerity in his voice made her throat tighten. She swallowed hard, blinking against the sudden sting of tears.

"You're giving me too much credit," she said quietly.

"Not nearly enough," Callum replied.

The day unfolded in a series of small victories. The final repairs were completed, the last bit of furniture placed just so. By afternoon, Isla and Callum stood on the front porch, surveying the inn with a shared sense of accomplishment.

"You know," Callum said, leaning against the railing, "I think The Tidesong's ready for guests."

Isla laughed softly, the sound light with relief. "It's ready for a lot of things."

"And you?" he asked, his voice dipping into something softer. "Are you ready?"

She turned to him, her heart pounding at the weight of his question. "For what?"

"For whatever's next," he said, his gaze steady.

Isla hesitated, the fear of uncertainty tugging at her edges. But then she looked at him—the quiet strength in his eyes, the unwavering support he'd given her—and the answer became clear.

"I think I am," she said, her voice soft but sure.

Callum's smile was small but full of promise. "Good. Because I'm sticking around for it."

That evening, Isla found herself once again on the cliffs, the sea stretching endlessly before her. She held her father's compass in her hand, the weight of it familiar and comforting.

Her grandmother's words echoed in her mind. Rebuild it. Make it yours.

The Tidesong wasn't just her family's legacy anymore—it was her own. A place she could anchor herself, a place where new memories could be made.

Footsteps approached behind her, and she turned to see Callum, his hands tucked into his pockets.

"Thought I'd find you here," he said, his voice warm.

"It's my thinking spot," Isla replied with a small smile.

Callum stepped beside her, his gaze sweeping over the waves. "What are you thinking about?"

She looked down at the compass, then back at him. "How far I've come. How much this place has given me. And how much I don't want to lose it."

"You won't," he said firmly.

Isla hesitated, then reached for his hand, her fingers threading through his. "And what about you? What are you thinking?"

He smiled, his grip on her hand tightening slightly. "That I'm exactly where I'm supposed to be."

Isla's chest ached with the beauty of the moment, the quiet certainty that, for the first time, she wasn't standing on the edge of something uncertain—she was standing at the beginning of something extraordinary.

As the waves crashed below and the stars began to scatter across the sky, Isla leaned into Callum, letting the rhythm of the sea guide her forward.

Chapter Sixteen: The Grand Opening

The morning of The Tidesong's reopening dawned bright and clear, the sunlight spilling across the freshly painted walls and sparkling windows. The inn stood proud and gleaming, ready to welcome guests for the first time in over a decade.

Isla stood at the front desk, adjusting the arrangement of fresh flowers Lila had brought in from the garden. The lavender and daisies added a cheerful touch, their soft colors complementing the warm hues of the inn's interior.

She caught her reflection in the polished mirror hanging behind the desk. Her eyes lingered on her face—not for vanity, but in quiet recognition. She looked different, lighter. Stronger.

A sound from the porch broke her reverie, and she turned to see Callum entering, his sleeves rolled up and a satisfied grin on his face.

"The sign's officially up," he announced.

"The Tidesong Inn," Isla said, savoring the name. "It feels real now."

"It's more than real," Callum replied. "It's ready."

The first guests began arriving just before noon, a mix of travelers and locals curious to see the inn's transformation. Isla greeted each one with a genuine smile, her nerves replaced by excitement as she watched the rooms fill with life and laughter.

Mrs. Hensley stopped by with a platter of homemade pastries, which she set on the coffee table in the parlor. "You've done something remarkable here, Isla," she said, her voice warm.

"Thank you," Isla replied, her chest swelling with pride.

As the afternoon unfolded, the inn hummed with energy. Children ran through the garden, their laughter echoing in the air. Couples lingered in the parlor, sipping tea and admiring the carefully restored furniture. The Tidesong was alive again, its heart beating strong.

Later that evening, as the guests settled in, Isla and Callum stood on the back porch, watching the last traces of sunlight dip below the horizon.

"You did it," Callum said, his voice filled with quiet pride.

"We did it," Isla corrected, glancing at him with a soft smile.

Callum shook his head. "I just helped with the heavy lifting. You're the one who brought this place back to life."

Isla turned to him, her eyes shining. "It wouldn't have happened without you, Callum. I hope you know that."

He looked at her, his expression steady but full of something deeper. "I'm just glad I got to be a part of it."

Their gazes held for a moment, the air between them charged with unspoken words.

"Stay," Isla said suddenly, her voice barely above a whisper.

Callum's brow furrowed. "What do you mean?"

"I mean... here. With me. At The Tidesong." She hesitated, her heart pounding. "You've been part of this place from the start. It wouldn't feel right without you."

A slow smile spread across Callum's face. "You're asking me to move in?"

"I'm asking you to stay," Isla clarified, her cheeks flushing.

Callum reached for her hand, his grip firm and grounding. "I wasn't planning on going anywhere."

Isla let out a soft laugh, the sound tinged with relief and joy. "Good."

The waves crashed below, their rhythm steady and unyielding, as Callum pulled her closer, his hand brushing her cheek. Their kiss was soft, unhurried, filled with the quiet promise of all that lay ahead.

For the first time in years, Isla felt like she was exactly where she was meant to be.

The Tidesong wasn't just a place—it was a home.
And now, it was theirs.

Chapter Seventeen: Tides of Belonging

The days following the grand opening of The Tidesong Inn passed in a blur of joyful chaos. Guests came and went, their laughter and stories weaving into the walls of the old inn, breathing new life into its foundation. For Isla, it was everything she had dreamed of—and more.

Mornings were filled with the scent of fresh coffee and baked goods, the sounds of footsteps on polished wood, and the occasional peal of laughter drifting from the garden. Evenings brought quiet conversations in the parlor, soft music playing from the old piano in the corner, and the flickering glow of lanterns casting warm light across the porch.

It wasn't just an inn anymore—it was a sanctuary.

One afternoon, Isla found herself in the kitchen with Lila, the little girl perched on a stool as she concentrated on frosting a batch of cupcakes. Her tongue peeked out in concentration, and her small hands were steady as she spread the icing.

"You're getting really good at that," Isla said, leaning against the counter and watching her work.

Lila beamed, glancing up. "Dad says practice makes perfect."

"He's not wrong," Isla replied, smiling.

Lila hesitated, then asked, "Do you think people like staying here because it feels... happy?"

Isla blinked, taken aback by the question. "I think so. Why do you ask?"

"Because it didn't feel happy before," Lila said matter-of-factly. "But now it does. And I like it."

Isla's heart swelled, and she reached out to brush a stray curl from Lila's forehead. "I like it too, kiddo."

Later that day, Isla walked through the garden, inspecting the newly planted flowers. Callum was repairing a section of the fence near the edge of the property, his sleeves rolled up and his focus intense. She paused to watch him, her chest tightening with a quiet, unshakable affection.

"Don't just stand there," Callum called without looking up. "You're making me nervous."

Isla laughed, crossing her arms. "I didn't realize watching you work was a crime."

"It is when you're judging my technique," he teased, straightening and wiping his hands on his jeans.

She grinned, closing the distance between them. "I wasn't judging. I was admiring."

Callum raised an eyebrow, his lips quirking. "Admiring, huh?"

"Don't let it go to your head," Isla said, though her smile softened the words.

Callum leaned against the fence, his eyes scanning the garden before settling on her. "You've done something incredible here, Isla. It's not just the inn—it's you. The way you've brought people together, made this place a home again."

She looked down, her cheeks warming. "I didn't do it alone."

"No," he agreed. "But you were the one who made it possible."

For a moment, they stood in comfortable silence, the breeze rustling the leaves around them. Then Callum reached out, brushing a strand of hair from Isla's face.

"You belong here," he said softly.

Isla looked up at him, her chest tight with emotion. "So do you."

Callum's smile deepened, his hand lingering against her cheek. "Good thing I'm not going anywhere."

That evening, as the guests settled in for the night, Isla and Callum sat on the porch, their chairs side by side. The moon cast a silvery glow over the cliffs, and the sound of the waves filled the quiet between them.

"I think I finally understand what my grandmother meant," Isla said, her voice low.

"About what?" Callum asked, turning to her.

"About this place being a legacy," she replied. "It's not just about the past—it's about what we build now, what we leave for the future."

Callum nodded, his gaze thoughtful. "And what are you going to leave?"

Isla looked out at the horizon, the compass heavy in her pocket. "Something worth remembering," she said softly.

Callum reached for her hand, his grip warm and steady. "You already have."

Isla turned to him, her heart full. She didn't have all the answers, and there were still pieces of the past she might never fully understand. But here, in this moment, she felt whole.

The Tidesong was alive again, its walls holding not just memories but the promise of a future filled with love, laughter, and belonging.

And as the waves crashed below, Isla knew she was exactly where she was meant to be.

Chapter Eighteen: The Keeper's Promise

The days melted into weeks, and The Tidesong Inn became more than just a landmark in Windhaven—it became a hub of life. Locals brought friends and family to share stories in its parlor, while travelers sought its charm for quiet escapes. It was everything Isla had hoped it could be.

But as much as the inn thrived, Isla's mind often returned to the unopened chapters of her father's story. The ledger, the letters, and the mysterious legacy tied to the inn still tugged at her thoughts like a whisper carried on the wind.

One evening, as the last of the guests retired to their rooms and the inn settled into quiet, Isla found herself in the attic again. She pulled the journal and the letters from their hiding place and spread them across the floor, lit by the faint glow of a desk lamp.

Her father's words stared back at her, the lines heavy with regret and longing. Trust the sea. The phrase had guided her for weeks, urging her forward, but now it felt like a riddle she still couldn't solve.

"What are you looking for?" Callum's voice came from the doorway, startling her.

She turned to see him leaning against the frame, his expression curious but gentle.

"I'm not sure," she admitted, sitting back on her heels. "There's so much I still don't understand about my dad, about what he was trying to do here. I feel like I've only scratched the surface."

Callum stepped into the room, crouching beside her. "Maybe it's not about finding all the answers. Maybe it's about what you do with what you know."

Isla tilted her head, considering his words. "What do you mean?"

"You've already rebuilt the inn, Isla," he said. "You've given it new life. Maybe that's the real legacy he wanted for you—not the past, but the future."

The weight of his words settled over her, and for the first time, she felt a flicker of peace. Maybe Callum was right. Maybe the answers she sought weren't about understanding every detail of her father's choices but about honoring the heart of what he'd tried to protect.

The next day, Isla took the ledger and letters to her grandmother. They sat together in the cozy warmth of Eleanor's bungalow, the afternoon light streaming through the windows.

"I want to make sure these stay safe," Isla said, placing the items on the table between them. "They're part of our history, and I don't want to lose that."

Eleanor nodded, her eyes glistening with pride. "You've done more than I ever could have hoped, Isla. Your father would be proud of you."

The words hit Isla like a wave, and she blinked back tears. "I hope so," she said softly.

Eleanor reached out, squeezing Isla's hand. "He loved you more than anything. Don't ever doubt that."

That evening, back at the inn, Isla stood in the garden, the sea breeze brushing against her skin. Callum joined her a moment later, his presence as steady as the tide.

"Your grandmother okay?" he asked.

"She is," Isla replied. "I think she's finally at peace with everything. And maybe I am too."

Callum's hand brushed hers, his fingers threading through hers with quiet certainty. "So what's next?"

Isla looked out at the horizon, her chest swelling with a mix of hope and determination. "I think it's time to write the next chapter."

Callum smiled, his grip on her hand tightening slightly. "Whatever it is, you won't be doing it alone."

Isla turned to him, her heart full as she leaned into his warmth. "I know."

As the waves crashed below and the stars began to scatter across the night sky, Isla felt the truth settle deep in her chest: the past had shaped her, but the future was hers to create.

The Tidesong was no longer just a legacy to preserve—it was a life to live.

And with Callum by her side, it was a life she was ready to embrace.

Chapter Nineteen: A Legacy Reborn

Autumn settled over Windhaven, painting the cliffs and town in rich hues of amber and gold. The mornings were cool and crisp, with a faint mist rolling in from the sea, and the afternoons were bathed in the gentle warmth of the season's dwindling sunlight.

At The Tidesong, the inn continued to thrive. Guests arrived from neighboring towns and far-off cities, drawn by the stories of its revival. They spoke of the inn's charm, of its warmth and the sense of peace it seemed to offer. Isla often overheard snippets of their conversations as she moved through the halls, and each one left her chest swelling with quiet pride.

One evening, after the last guest had checked in and the house had settled into a peaceful hum, Isla found herself in the parlor. A fire crackled in the hearth, casting soft shadows across the room. She ran her fingers along the spines of the books on the shelf, many of them left behind by her grandmother.

Callum entered, carrying two mugs of tea. He handed one to her, his fingers brushing hers as he did.

"Busy day," he said, settling into the armchair by the fire.

"Always is," Isla replied, taking a seat on the sofa opposite him. "Not that I'm complaining."

Callum smiled, his gaze lingering on her. "You seem different."

"Different how?" she asked, tilting her head.

"Lighter," he said simply.

Isla considered his words, her mind drifting to the months that had passed since she'd returned to Windhaven. The weight she'd carried for so long—the pain of her father's absence, the uncertainty of her place in the world—had eased.

"I think I am," she admitted. "For the first time in a long time, I feel like I'm where I'm supposed to be."

Callum's smile deepened, and the warmth in his eyes made her chest tighten. "You've come a long way."

"So have you," she said, her voice soft.

He raised an eyebrow. "Me?"

"You're not exactly the same grumpy contractor I met on my first night here," Isla teased.

Callum chuckled, shaking his head. "I was never grumpy. You just caught me on a bad day."

"Right," she said, her tone playful. "You're all sunshine and rainbows."

"Exactly," he replied, his smirk widening.

They laughed together, the sound filling the room with a warmth that rivaled the fire. For a moment, the world outside the inn seemed to fade away, leaving only the two of them and the quiet promise of what they were building together.

As autumn gave way to winter, the inn adapted. Guests arrived seeking the cozy charm of its roaring fires and soft blankets, the perfect retreat from the chilly sea winds. Isla loved watching the transformation, loved seeing how the seasons breathed new life into the place she had fought so hard to restore.

One evening, as snow began to fall outside, Callum joined her on the back porch. They stood side by side, their breath visible in the cold air, the sea below a dark, restless expanse.

"You've built something incredible here," Callum said, his voice quiet but firm.

"It's not just me," Isla replied, her gaze fixed on the horizon.

"Maybe not," he said, turning to her. "But you're the heart of it."

Isla felt her cheeks warm, and she looked down, the weight of his words settling over her.

"I couldn't have done it without you," she said, her voice soft. "You've been here every step of the way."

"And I'm not going anywhere," Callum said, his tone steady.

She turned to him, her chest tightening. "Good."

The words were simple, but they carried a depth that neither of them could ignore.

Callum reached for her hand, his fingers warm against hers. "I mean it, Isla. Whatever comes next, we'll face it together."

Isla smiled, her heart full. For the first time in years, she wasn't afraid of what the future might hold.

The Tidesong was more than just an inn now—it was a symbol of resilience, of hope, of love. And with Callum by her side, Isla knew she was exactly where she was meant to be.

As the snow fell around them, soft and silent, Isla leaned into him, her heart anchored in the promise of everything yet to come.

Chapter Twenty: Tides of Forever

The winter sun rose late over Windhaven, its light a pale gold that bathed The Tidesong in a gentle glow. Snow dusted the rooftops and garden paths, softening the edges of the world. Inside, the inn buzzed with quiet energy—guests chatting over steaming mugs of coffee, Lila skipping between tables with a plate of freshly baked scones, and the crackling of a fire in the parlor.

Isla stood at the front desk, checking the day's schedule. Her movements were automatic, but her mind drifted. The inn had become everything she had hoped for—alive, vibrant, a place where memories were made and shared.

But today felt different.

The air held a sense of anticipation, as if the tides themselves were shifting.

Later that afternoon, Callum found her in the garden, carefully clearing the snow from the lavender beds. He leaned against the porch railing, watching her with a faint smile.

"You know you don't have to do that," he said.

Isla glanced up, brushing a stray curl from her face. "I like taking care of them. They remind me of what this place has been through. How it's grown."

Callum's smile deepened as he stepped closer, his boots crunching softly on the snow. "Kind of like someone else I know."

Isla raised an eyebrow, her lips quirking. "Are you trying to flatter me, Callum Drake?"

"Maybe," he said, his tone teasing but warm.

She laughed, the sound light and unguarded, before turning back to her work. Callum crouched beside her, his hands brushing hers as he helped clear the last of the snow.

"Isla," he said quietly, his voice soft but steady.

She turned to him, her heart skipping at the look in his eyes. "What?"

Callum hesitated, then reached into his pocket and pulled out a small velvet box. Isla froze, her breath catching as he opened it to reveal a delicate silver ring, the design simple yet elegant.

"I've been carrying this around for a while now," he said, his voice thick with emotion. "Waiting for the right moment."

Her eyes filled with tears as he continued, his gaze never leaving hers.

"You've rebuilt this place, Isla. You've rebuilt yourself. And somewhere along the way, you rebuilt me too. I can't imagine my life without you. I don't want to."

Isla's hand flew to her mouth, her chest tight with disbelief and overwhelming joy.

"So I'm asking you," Callum said, his voice breaking slightly, "to let me stay. Not just here at The Tidesong, but with you. Forever."

The world seemed to hold its breath as Isla stared at him, her tears spilling over.

"Yes," she whispered, her voice trembling but certain. "Yes, Callum."

Relief and joy broke over his face as he slid the ring onto her finger, his hands steady despite the emotion radiating from him. He pulled her into his arms, holding her close as the snow fell softly around them.

When their lips met, it was a kiss filled with promises—of love, of laughter, of a future built together.

That evening, the inn buzzed with excitement as word of their engagement spread among the guests. Lila was the most exuberant of all, spinning in circles around the parlor as she declared herself "chief flower girl."

Isla watched it all with a full heart, her hand resting lightly over Callum's.

"This place feels different now," she said softly.

"It's because it's finally whole," Callum replied, his voice filled with quiet certainty.

Isla smiled, leaning her head against his shoulder. The Tidesong had been her family's legacy, a place tied to her past. But now it was also a place of hope, of healing, of love.

And as the waves crashed against the cliffs below, Isla knew with unwavering certainty that her life was no longer defined by what she had lost.

It was defined by what she had found.

Chapter Twenty-One: A Life in Bloom

Spring returned to Windhaven, its arrival heralded by bursts of color in the garden and the warm hum of the sea breeze. The Tidesong Inn stood as a beacon of life, its charm spreading through the town like the first blush of dawn.

The inn had flourished under Isla's care, its reputation growing with every guest who passed through its doors. Yet for Isla, the most cherished moments were not the bustling mornings or the lively evenings. They were the quiet ones, shared with Callum and Lila, where laughter mingled with the sounds of the waves and life felt impossibly full.

On a particularly bright afternoon, Isla found herself in the garden, planting a new row of lavender. The soil was warm beneath her hands, and the scent of fresh earth mingled with the saltiness of the sea air. She heard footsteps behind her and turned to see Lila bounding toward her, clutching a small bouquet of wildflowers.

"Look what I found!" Lila exclaimed, her smile as radiant as the sun.

"They're beautiful," Isla said, brushing her hands off and taking the flowers.

"Dad says we should put them in the dining room," Lila added, bouncing on her toes. "For the guests."

Isla smiled, glancing toward the porch where Callum stood, watching them with an expression that made her heart swell.

"That's a great idea," she said, ruffling Lila's curls. "Let's do it."

Inside, the inn was a hive of quiet activity. Guests chatted over tea in the parlor, and soft music played from the vintage record player Isla had restored with Callum's help. The dining room glowed with natural light, the vases of wildflowers adding a cheerful touch to the tables.

Callum joined Isla at the front desk, his hand brushing against hers as he leaned over the guest book. "We're fully booked for the weekend," he said, his tone light.

"That's a first," Isla said, grinning.

"Won't be the last," Callum replied, his smile warm.

She looked at him, her heart full. "We've come a long way, haven't we?"

Callum met her gaze, his expression steady. "And we're just getting started."

That evening, Isla and Callum sat on the back porch, the garden bathed in the soft glow of string lights. Lila had fallen asleep upstairs, her laughter still echoing in the air.

Isla leaned back in her chair, the warmth of Callum's hand in hers grounding her. The sea stretched before them, vast and endless, its rhythm a constant reminder of life's ebb and flow.

"Do you ever think about what's next?" Isla asked, her voice soft.

Callum turned to her, his eyes thoughtful. "What do you mean?"

"For us," she said, her gaze drifting to the horizon. "We've rebuilt this place. We've made it ours. But what comes after?"

Callum was quiet for a moment, then squeezed her hand gently. "I think what comes next is what we decide to build together. A life. A family. Whatever you want, Isla."

Her breath caught, and she turned to him, her chest tight with emotion. "A family," she repeated, the words both terrifying and exhilarating.

Callum smiled, his gaze unwavering. "If that's what you want."

Isla looked out at the garden, at the lights that swayed gently in the breeze, and felt the undeniable pull of something bigger than herself.

"I think it is," she said, her voice steady. "I think I want all of it."

Callum's smile deepened, and he leaned in, pressing a soft kiss to her temple. "Then that's what we'll have."

The seasons continued to turn, each one bringing new life and new beginnings to The Tidesong. The inn became a place where stories were shared and new ones began, where love and laughter filled every corner.

And as Isla stood on the cliffs one evening, watching the sun set over the sea, she felt the unshakable certainty that her life—like the inn—had become a home.

The Tidesong wasn't just her legacy.

It was her future.

Chapter Twenty-Two: The Rising Tide

Summer arrived at Windhaven with a breathless energy, the town bustling with visitors and life. The Tidesong Inn became the heart of the activity, its rooms filled with guests who returned year after year, drawn not just by the beauty of the place but by the warmth of Isla and the stories the inn held within its walls.

For Isla, life had settled into a rhythm she hadn't dared to dream of before. The inn was thriving, the garden was in full bloom, and her days were spent surrounded by laughter, love, and a future she was building one step at a time.

One morning, as Isla sat on the porch with a cup of coffee, Lila burst through the front door, a piece of paper clutched in her hand.

"Isla! Look what I made!" she exclaimed, holding up a brightly colored drawing.

Isla took the paper, her smile widening as she studied it. The drawing depicted The Tidesong, complete with its green trim and the lavender beds, under a bright yellow sun. At the center stood three stick figures labeled "Me," "Dad," and "Isla."

"It's perfect," Isla said, ruffling Lila's curls.

Lila grinned. "You're going to put it on the wall, right? Where everyone can see it?"

"Of course," Isla said.

Callum appeared in the doorway, a mug in his hand and an amused look on his face. "I see I've been roped into being a work of art."

"You're famous now," Isla teased, holding up the drawing.

Callum chuckled, leaning against the doorframe. "Guess I'll have to live up to it."

That afternoon, as the inn bustled with guests, Isla found herself in the garden with Eleanor. Her grandmother sat in a wicker chair, her sharp eyes watching Isla as she tended to the lavender.

"You've done well," Eleanor said, her voice softer than usual.

Isla glanced up, surprised. "Thank you."

Eleanor's gaze swept over the garden, the inn, and the sea beyond. "Your father would be proud of you."

The words landed like a gift, warming Isla's chest. She set down her tools and moved to sit beside Eleanor, taking her hand.

"I think I finally understand what he was trying to do," Isla said. "Why he left, why he cared so much about this place."

Eleanor nodded, her expression thoughtful. "The Tidesong was always more than just a building. It was a part of him, of us. And now it's a part of you, too."

Isla squeezed her grandmother's hand. "I just hope I can honor that."

"You already have," Eleanor said, her voice firm.

That evening, as the sun dipped below the horizon, Isla and Callum stood on the cliffs, the compass nestled in Isla's hand. She turned it over, the familiar weight grounding her.

"I've been thinking," Isla said, breaking the comfortable silence.

"Uh-oh," Callum teased, his tone light.

She nudged him playfully before continuing. "I want to add something to the inn—a place where people can leave pieces of themselves. Stories, memories. Something that ties everyone who comes through here to this place."

Callum considered her words, his gaze thoughtful. "Like a guestbook, but more personal?"

"Exactly," Isla said. "A legacy for The Tidesong, built by the people who stay here."

Callum smiled, the warmth in his eyes making her chest ache. "I think that's a perfect idea."

They stood in silence for a moment, the waves crashing below. Then Callum reached for her hand, his grip firm and steady.

"You've got a way of making things feel bigger than they are," he said softly.

Isla looked up at him, her heart full. "That's because they are."

Callum leaned in, his lips brushing hers in a kiss that spoke of all they had built together and everything that still lay ahead.

The next day, Isla began setting up what she called "The Memory Room." It was a small, sunlit space near the back of the inn, filled with empty journals, photo frames, and small boxes where guests could leave mementos. She explained the idea to the first group of guests, who embraced it with enthusiasm.

By the end of the week, the room was already filling with letters, photos, and tiny trinkets—tokens of love, gratitude, and memories forged at The Tidesong.

Isla stood in the doorway one evening, watching as a young couple placed a photograph of themselves in one of the frames. The sight filled her with a quiet pride, the kind that reminded her why she had fought so hard to bring the inn back to life.

"This place keeps growing," Callum said, appearing beside her.

"Because it's alive," Isla replied.

He smiled, wrapping an arm around her shoulders. "Just like you."

Isla leaned into him, her heart full. The Tidesong wasn't just a legacy anymore. It was a living, breathing testament to the resilience of love, the power of belonging, and the beauty of new beginnings.

And as the waves sang their endless song below, Isla knew that the tide of her life had truly turned.

Chapter Twenty-Three: A Future Etched in Stone

The sun hung low over Windhaven, casting long shadows across the cliffs and painting The Tidesong in hues of gold. The inn stood proud, its windows glinting like jewels in the warm light. Inside, the hum of life continued—a blend of laughter, footsteps, and the soft murmurs of guests savoring the serenity of their stay.

For Isla, the rhythm of the inn had become second nature. Every morning brought new faces, new stories, and new memories to add to the growing legacy she was building.

But today felt different. Today marked the culmination of everything she had worked for since she first returned to Windhaven.

The Memory Room was complete. The walls were lined with shelves of journals filled with handwritten notes, photographs, and trinkets left by guests. It was a space brimming with life and love, a living archive of all that The Tidesong had come to mean.

Isla stood in the doorway, her heart swelling as she ran her fingers over the nearest shelf. Each entry, each keepsake, was a testament to the spirit of the inn—a reminder that it was not just a place but a home for everyone who passed through its doors.

Callum appeared behind her, his presence steady and grounding. "You did it," he said, his voice filled with quiet pride.

"We did it," Isla corrected, turning to him with a smile.

He reached out, brushing a strand of hair from her face. "What's next?"

Isla hesitated, her gaze drifting to the horizon visible through the window. "I think it's time to make this official," she said, her voice firm.

"What do you mean?" Callum asked, tilting his head.

"I mean creating something permanent," Isla said. "Something that ties The Tidesong to everything it's become."

The next week was a whirlwind of planning and preparation. Isla enlisted the help of local artists and craftspeople to create a permanent tribute to The Tidesong's legacy. Together, they designed a stone mosaic to be placed in the garden—a sprawling piece that depicted the inn, the cliffs, and the sea, interwoven with symbols and words inspired by the stories left in the Memory Room.

Guests and townspeople alike pitched in, contributing pieces of colored glass, shells, and stones to be incorporated into the design. The project became a communal effort, a celebration of the connection The Tidesong had fostered among its visitors and the community.

On the day the mosaic was unveiled, the garden was filled with people. Neighbors, guests, and friends gathered under the afternoon sun, their voices blending into a joyful chorus.

Isla stood at the center of it all, her heart pounding as she prepared to speak. Callum stood beside her, his steady presence giving her the courage she needed.

"Thank you all for being here," Isla began, her voice carrying over the crowd. "When I first came back to Windhaven, I wasn't sure what I'd find—or what I was looking for. But what I discovered was more than I could have imagined."

She paused, her eyes scanning the faces of those who had become a part of her journey. "The Tidesong has always been more than just a building. It's a place where stories are shared, where connections are made, and where memories are built. This mosaic is our way of honoring that legacy and everyone who's been a part of it."

With that, she gestured for the cloth covering the mosaic to be pulled away. Gasps and cheers erupted as the intricate design was revealed, the sunlight catching the shimmering glass and shells.

The mosaic was beautiful, a vibrant testament to The Tidesong's history and its future. At its center were three words etched in stone: Love, Belonging, Resilience.

That evening, as the last of the guests trickled inside and the garden grew quiet, Isla and Callum stood before the mosaic, the moonlight casting a silvery glow over its surface.

"You've created something extraordinary," Callum said, his voice soft.

"We did," Isla replied, reaching for his hand.

He turned to her, his gaze steady. "You've built more than an inn, Isla. You've built a home—for yourself, for Lila, for everyone who steps through these doors."

Isla smiled, her chest tightening with gratitude. "And for you," she said, her voice barely above a whisper.

Callum leaned in, his forehead resting against hers. "Always for me."

The waves crashed against the cliffs below, their rhythm a familiar comfort. Isla closed her eyes, letting the sound wash over her as Callum's arms wrapped around her.

The Tidesong wasn't just a legacy anymore. It was a promise. A place where love would always find its way, where belonging was etched in every stone, and where resilience was the tide that carried them forward.

And as Isla stood there, held in the warmth of Callum's embrace, she knew that her life had finally come full circle.

Chapter Twenty-Four: Everlasting Tides

Autumn returned to Windhaven, its golden light spilling over the cliffs and painting the sea in hues of amber and bronze. The Tidesong Inn hummed with life, the sound of footsteps on polished floors mingling with laughter and the rustle of leaves carried by the wind.

For Isla, every season at The Tidesong brought new stories, new memories, and a deeper sense of belonging. The inn had become a living, breathing testament to resilience and love, and every person who passed through its doors left a part of themselves behind.

But this autumn was special. It marked the first anniversary of the inn's reopening, a milestone Isla had once only dreamed of reaching.

The day of the anniversary celebration was clear and crisp, the air tinged with the scent of salt and lavender. The garden was alive with color, its paths lined with golden mums and bright marigolds. Lanterns swayed gently in the breeze, their soft light casting a warm glow over the gathering crowd.

Isla moved through the garden, greeting guests and ensuring everything was in place. Lila darted past her, a crown of autumn leaves perched on her curls as she handed out small lavender bouquets to the guests.

Callum appeared beside her, his hands in his pockets and a soft smile on his lips. "Everything looks perfect," he said, his voice filled with quiet pride.

Isla smiled back, her chest tightening with emotion. "It does, doesn't it?"

Callum nodded toward the garden's center, where the mosaic shimmered under the afternoon light. "That's your heart right there. Everything this place stands for."

Isla followed his gaze, her smile softening. The mosaic had become the heart of The Tidesong, a symbol of everything it had come to mean—not just to her, but to the community it now served.

As the sun began to set, Isla stood on the porch, her heart full as she addressed the crowd gathered below.

"A year ago, I came back to Windhaven unsure of what I'd find," she began, her voice steady despite the emotion welling in her chest. "But what I discovered was more than I could have imagined. The Tidesong isn't just a place—it's a home. And it's because of all of you that it's become what it is today."

The crowd cheered, their warmth and support washing over her. Isla glanced at Callum, who stood beside her, his gaze steady and full of pride.

"This inn has always been about connection," Isla continued. "About love, belonging, and resilience. And I can't wait to see how it continues to grow."

As the applause swelled, Isla felt a sense of peace settle over her. She had found her place, her purpose, and her people.

That evening, after the last guest had left and the lanterns flickered softly in the garden, Isla and Callum sat on the porch, the sound of the waves filling the quiet between them.

"You did it," Callum said, his hand resting over hers.

"We did it," Isla replied, her voice soft but sure.

Callum turned to her, his eyes shining with love. "What's next?"

Isla smiled, her gaze drifting toward the horizon. "Whatever we want," she said. "This place is ours now, and so is the future."

He leaned in, pressing a soft kiss to her forehead. "I like the sound of that."

Isla closed her eyes, letting the warmth of his embrace and the rhythm of the waves carry her forward.

The Tidesong wasn't just a legacy anymore. It was a life, a love, and a promise of everything yet to come.

And as the tide ebbed and flowed below, Isla knew with unwavering certainty that the best was still ahead.

Chapter Twenty-Five: Forever in the Tides

The winds of winter rolled gently into Windhaven, the sea's rhythm a steady heartbeat against the cliffs. Snow dusted The Tidesong Inn, its green trim standing out against the pristine white. Inside, the inn was alive with warmth: the soft glow of candles, the crackling fire in the parlor, and the hum of laughter and conversation from its many guests.

Isla stood by the Memory Room, her hand resting lightly on the doorframe. Over the past year, the small space had become her favorite corner of the inn. It was a mosaic of its own now—a growing collection of letters, photographs, and keepsakes left by guests. It wasn't just a room; it was the soul of The Tidesong.

As she moved to straighten a few of the items on the shelves, Lila appeared at her side, holding a shiny ornament shaped like a tiny seashell.

"Look!" Lila exclaimed, bouncing on her toes. "Dad and I made this for the tree!"

Isla crouched to take the ornament, her heart swelling at the sight of the intricate design. "It's beautiful, Lila. I think it's going to be the prettiest ornament on the whole tree."

Lila grinned, her curls bouncing as she spun on her heel. "I'll go put it on right now!"

As she dashed off, Isla felt Callum's presence before she heard him. His hand brushed her shoulder, grounding her as always.

"She's been planning that ornament for weeks," he said, his voice filled with warmth.

"It's perfect," Isla replied, turning to him. "She's perfect."

"She has a pretty good role model," Callum said, his eyes soft as they met hers.

Isla's breath caught, and she reached for his hand. "So do I."

That evening, as snow began to fall outside, Isla and Callum stood in the parlor, watching as Lila carefully hung the seashell ornament on the Christmas tree. The room was filled with guests, their voices a cheerful hum as they admired the decorations and exchanged stories by the fire.

The Tidesong felt more alive than ever, its walls a testament to the love and laughter that had been poured into it.

Callum slipped an arm around Isla's waist, pulling her closer. "You've built something incredible here," he said softly, his lips brushing her temple.

"We built it," Isla corrected, her voice steady.

His smile deepened, and he rested his forehead against hers. "I'm glad I stayed."

"Me too," Isla whispered, her chest tightening with love.

As the night grew quieter and the guests retired to their rooms, Isla and Callum found themselves alone on the back porch. The snow had stopped, leaving the world blanketed in white. The sea shimmered under the light of the moon, its surface calm and steady.

Callum reached into his pocket, pulling out the familiar compass he had given her when they'd first started working on the inn together. He placed it in her hand, his gaze serious but warm.

"You've always had the compass," he said. "Now, I think it's time you let it guide you to something new."

Isla looked down at the compass, her heart swelling with emotion. "I think it already has."

Callum cupped her face, his thumb brushing against her cheek. "Then let's keep going. Together."

Isla smiled, leaning into his touch. "Always."

The waves sang their endless song below, and for the first time in her life, Isla felt not just at home but whole.

The Tidesong was no longer just a legacy, no longer just a place to restore. It was her forever—a life built with love, shaped by resilience, and carried forward by the endless rhythm of the tides.

And as the stars sparkled above, Isla knew that the story of The Tidesong Inn—and the life they were building together—was only just beginning.

Also by Kenneth Thomas

Harrow Harbor Mysteries
Whispering Harbor Mystery
The Secret of the Cavern
The Ghost Ships Shadow

Moonlight Pact series
The Moonlight Pact
The Rift Redemption
The Riftbound Legacy

The Awakening Thread Chronicles
The Awakening Thread

The Broke Kids Club
The Broke Kids Club
The Broke Kids Club: Ripples of Change

The Broke Kids Club Collection
The Broke Kids Club Collection

The Convergence of Minds series
The Digital Agora: A Philosophical Epic of AI and Humanity
Foundation of the Agora
Beyond the Agora: Fractured Realms

The Echoes of Eternity
The Awakening of Nephira
The Rift Of Worlds

The Eclipse Chronicles
Shards of Light
Eclipse Reaver
Axis Reforged

The Veil of Shadows Series
Shattered Dominion
The Fractured Path

Standalone
A Tail of Darkness To Light

The Mirror Within
Echoes of Ink and Heart
Purpose Over Power: The Visionary Path of Servant Leadership
The Questions That Shape Us: Finding Life's Wisdom-The Power of
Inquiry
Where the Shadows Settle
30 Days to Inner Freedom: A Mindful Journey in Addiction Recovery
Towards a Sustainable Future: The UN's 17 Goals
Echoes of Becoming
Cognitive Freedom: The Stoic Path to Resilience and Recovery
Beneath the Cypress Sky
The Unbroken Pen
Where Tides Meet